A FATAL LIAISON

Irish detectives investigate a cold-blooded murder

DAVID PEARSON

THE BOOK FOLKS

Paperback edition published by

The Book Folks

London, 2020

ISBN 978-1-913516-91-8

www.thebookfolks.com

To Jimmy,
For reminding me that a sense of humour is essential.

Chapter One

Detective Inspector Aidan Burke was seated at his desk in Store Street Garda Station. It had been a busy week for the Gardaí. They had had all sorts to deal with from the usual robberies, suicides in the Liffey, drug seizures and quite a number of domestic assaults as well as a gangland shooting. With most of it in the process of being sorted out, Burke was enjoying a few minutes of relative peace. Then his phone rang.

"Burke," he said.

"Hello, Aidan. This is Superintendent Heffernan. Glad I caught you."

"Hello, sir. How can I help?"

"I've had a call from Tallaght. A car has gone into the ditch in a laneway off the N81. When the uniformed Gardaí were called out, they found what appears to be the driver dead at the wheel, but they're not happy that it was just an accident. They're very pressed today. There's some sort of demonstration going on at The Square. Could you drop out and lend a hand?"

"Yes, OK, sir. I'll go right away. Who should I contact for directions to the scene?" Burke said.

"Good man, Aidan. If you give Sergeant O'Grady a ring in Tallaght, he has the details. Oh, and keep me posted, won't you?"

"Yes, of course, sir. Talk later."

DI Aidan Burke had just recently turned fifty. He had contemplated retiring early from the force to try and get his life straightened out, but had been persuaded by his sergeant, Fiona Moore, not to take such a radical step. Since his divorce he had been drinking far too much, and generally not looking after himself. But when Moore discovered, quite by accident, that he was thinking of throwing in the towel, they had had a heart to heart and she had agreed to help him make some changes in his lifestyle. So far it was working. He had reduced his alcohol intake by about two-thirds, he had smartened up his appearance, and with Moore's help, had given his rather humble bachelor house in Crumlin a complete makeover.

Feeling more positive about life in general, he had agreed to postpone any decision about retirement for a couple of years to see how things went. He had to admit that he enjoyed being a relatively senior detective in Dublin, and he was good at his job. He had an excellent record, and although his methods were frequently controversial, to say the least, they were nevertheless effective.

* * *

Burke found Detective Sergeant Fiona Moore at her desk, updating the Garda PULSE system with details from the work that they had completed earlier in the week.

"C'mon, Sergeant, we need to go out," Burke said to her.

Moore locked the screen of her PC, grabbed her jacket from the back of her chair, and followed Burke out of the office.

On the way to the car park, Moore said to Burke, "What's the gig, boss?"

"Heffernan was on to me. There's some shit gone down between Tallaght and Blessington. I don't have many details, but it involves a car crash. Sergeant O'Grady from Tallaght is sending me the map reference."

"What do they need us for?" Moore said.

"Who knows. But I need to build some brownie points with Heffernan, so I'm not arguing, am I?"

"OK. Whatever."

Moore had joined the Gardaí some years back hoping to find a husband. She had been unlucky in love during her teen years, and on the advice of her mother, she had joined the force, where she was assured there were 'tons of hard-working, good-looking young men' to be had. She had lost some weight, and let her chestnut hair grow a good bit longer, so she was quite attractive by the time she arrived in Store Street from training in Templemore. Initially, she had hooked up with a more senior officer, but unbeknownst to her, he was already married, and when she found that out, she was furious. But she also found that she was enjoying the work quite a lot, so as time went by, she changed her objectives, being happier to focus on a career and set her romantic aspirations aside, at least temporarily.

Burke had recently acquired a new, unmarked Volvo S60. It was quite luxurious for a police car, but such a vehicle was necessary to keep up with the fancy hardware currently used by many criminals in and around Dublin.

It was mid-morning, and the early frost had thawed to a damp slickness on the city streets. As they drove out past Tallaght, they left behind the densely packed terraces and vast estates of small houses where the names of those who fought for Irish independence had been liberally scattered about in the form of street names. The men had been immortalized on the rectangular green and white signs affixed to the low walls at the entrance to the estates – Padraic Pearse Park, James Connolly Crescent and Michael Collins Road.

The land rose up steeply on the N81, and the terrain became quite densely wooded, with small patches of slowly thawing snow lying along the verges of the road where the trees were shading the grass. O'Grady had sent the co-ordinates of the location to Burke's phone, and it had appeared on the display in the centre console of his car, with directions being provided by Google Maps. Just before Gortnum Cottages, Burke turned right onto a narrow road known locally as McDonagh's Lane. After a few twists and turns, they came across an unmarked Ford Mondeo with blue flashing lights at the side of the road. A little further on there was a black BMW 5 Series that had left the road, and had hit a tree. Both the driver's and front passenger's doors of the stricken vehicle were open, but the car was badly smashed, the bonnet having folded upwards in a sharp inverted 'V', and the windscreen was cracked and crazed.

Burke brought his Volvo to a halt.

"Here we go," he said, getting out of the car.

The detectives walked over to where two uniformed Gardaí were standing, looking cold and a bit miserable, beside the damaged BMW.

Burke introduced himself and Moore, holding out his warrant card.

"Well, men, what's the story?"

"Good morning, sir; Sergeant. We were called out about an hour ago to this," the uniformed Garda said, gesturing to the BMW.

"At first, we thought it was just a straightforward car crash, but when we got to look at the driver, we began to think there was a bit more to it. He's been sick all over his clothes, and… well… sorry, sir, he's messed himself as well."

Burke leaned into the vehicle and examined the driver, who was slumped forward over the steering wheel. Burke placed two fingers against the man's neck, and determined that life had left him – there was no pulse. The driver was in his fifties, dressed smartly in a suit and tie, but his clothes were now soaked in vomit. His plentiful hair, going grey, was neatly cut, and his clothes weren't cheap. The interior of the car smelled strongly of cigar smoke, and there was a partly burnt, fat Havana in the ashtray, which had strangely stayed in place during the trauma.

Burke withdrew himself from the vehicle, feeling slightly nauseous.

"Have you run the number of the car?" he asked the young Garda standing close by.

"Eh, no, sir. We were waiting for someone to arrive," the man said rather sheepishly.

Having overheard Burke, Moore said, "I'm on it, boss. Just coming through now."

A moment later she spoke up again.

"The vehicle is registered to a Mr Gerald McCranny, and I have an address here too, but it looks like a business address," she said.

"Right. Better get on to O'Higgins, get his mob out then. These guys were right. This isn't just any old RTA."

Dr Malcolm O'Higgins was the state pathologist who worked with the Gardaí when dead bodies were found. He was a serious, humourless man in his late fifties, and he always wore a grey suit which matched his grey complexion. He never looked well fed, and his clothes hung limply on his emaciated frame to the extent that one wondered if he wasn't near death himself. However, he was a good pathologist. Totally thorough, and well used to finding tiny morsels of evidence that would have slipped past a more lackadaisical person – the Gardaí were pleased to have his dedicated services.

Moore made the call and reported that O'Higgins would be out within the hour along with two or three of his assistants. He urged the detectives not to interfere in any way with the body or the scene until he was on hand.

"Tell you what, lads. Why don't you two pop down to the village and get us all a nice hot cup of coffee and a few buns. Here – this should cover it," Burke said handing the young Garda standing nearby a €20 note.

The uniformed Garda didn't have to be asked twice. The two of them got into their blue Mondeo, turned it, and drove off towards Blessington in search of refreshments.

"Right, c'mon Fiona. Let's have a good look around before O'Higgins gets here."

Burke and Moore donned blue vinyl gloves and approached the BMW.

"You look in the back, and in the boot. I'll take the front," Burke said.

After a few minutes, Moore came around to where Burke was standing on the passenger's side of the car, leaning in, going through the contents of the glovebox.

"Aidan – I found this file on the back seat. Looks like something to do with construction."

"Good. There's bugger all up front, and it's not very nice in there. See if you can get a phone number from the file for his business and give them a call. Try and get his home number from them. There's no point in postponing the inevitable, I suppose. By the way, why do you think the passenger door is open?"

"Dunno. Maybe it sprang open in the crash," Moore said.

"Na, that's not the way it works. And look here – there are muddy footprints on the floor mat on that side. They look like trainers or something. Could there have been a passenger in the car?"

"Hmm… could have been, I suppose, but where did he go?"

"Search me, but we could have a murderer on the loose running around the Dublin Mountains – fabulous! Better get a gang of uniforms out to comb the area. Dogs too."

Moore got busy on her phone, getting whatever resources she could scrounge from the surrounding Garda stations.

As the morning wore on, a watery sun was trying to break through the thin clouds overhead to warm the land below. Moore had sat back into the relative heat of Burke's Volvo to make the calls.

Burke continued his exploration of the terrain around the crashed car. He made sure not to trample on any possible evidence, but he thought he could detect depressions in the soft ground leading away from the vehicle, where it looked as if someone might have taken off through the undergrowth and into the woods.

Chapter Two

By mid-morning the scene of the accident was buzzing. The two uniformed Gardaí – the first responders – had arrived back with hot drinks and donuts which had been eagerly consumed by Burke and Moore, who were feeling slightly warmer as a result. More squad cars arrived carrying one or two uniformed officers in each, and a small white van had turned up carrying a dog handler and a very alert-looking German shepherd dog.

Dr O'Higgins had arrived as well, and together with two assistants, now clad in white scene-of-crime suits, all three were probing the area in fine detail. One of the men had retrieved the driver's wallet from his inside jacket pocket. It contained several credit cards, a driving license and a passport card all in the name of Gerald McCranny. Both the driving license and the passport card had a photo of the deceased, putting the identity of the driver beyond doubt.

Burke approached the doctor.

"What's the story, Doctor?"

"The story, Inspector, is that you have dead body."

"Can you give us something more? Time of death? Cause of death?"

"Given the vomit, and the general state of the man, if you know what I mean, I'm not convinced that it was the crash that killed him. I need to do a proper examination – you know, bloods, toxicology, that sort of thing," O'Higgins said.

"Very well, Doctor. Let us know what you find."

Moore had been listening to the conversation between the doctor and her boss.

"What do you make of it, boss?" she said.

"I'm not sure yet. Why couldn't it just be a straightforward car crash? I'm bloody freezing here!" Burke said.

An all-black Mercedes van with 'City Morgue' written discreetly in gold lettering on the tailgate was parked nearby to receive the body, and a beaten-up old tow truck was standing off with its engine running to keep its occupants warm, ready to take the smashed BMW back to Tallaght Garda station where it would join several other crashed cars that were kept as evidence in other cases.

"Did you get an address for him?" Burke asked Moore.

"Yes, I did. Foxrock, no less."

Foxrock is a posh suburb on the south side of Dublin where housing is at its most expensive. There is a small village of the same name, but most of the area is now sprinkled with detached houses in their own grounds, and a few small, gated estates where the well-to-do of Dublin reside in quiet, peaceful surroundings.

"Strange thing is his house is called The Glebe. I thought that was religious or something," Moore said.

"It used to be. Land and buildings that were donated to the church in days gone by. But most of them are far too big these days, so they've been sold off. It's probably quite a nice old place. I wonder if he has much land."

"Dunno. We'll know soon enough."

Burke briefed a sergeant who had taken control of the search and the dog handler, asking them to keep him posted if anything of significance developed. Moore and himself set off to break the news to McCranny's family.

* * *

The Glebe was indeed a fine residence. Probably built in the latter part of the nineteenth century, and set in almost an acre of manicured lawns and gardens. The house was accessed via a pair of wrought iron gates standing open, set in granite pillars. A double-fronted building, in slightly austere grey stone, reflective of its original purpose, the house now boasted a bright yellow front door and had a large Mercedes 4x4 parked outside.

Burke drove in and brought his car to a halt on the gravel. They both got out and Burke rang the doorbell – a nice old ceramic bell push set in polished brass to the side of the entrance.

They could hear the bell ringing deep inside the house. Then came the unmistakeable sound of footsteps advancing up the hall and the door was opened by a thin, dark-haired woman in her mid-twenties dressed in a beige polo neck sweater and blue jeans.

"Mrs McCranny?" Moore enquired.

"Oh, no," the woman said, smiling, "she is in the kitchen. Who shall I say?"

Burke offered his warrant card, and the girl became very serious, turning away and heading back down the long central corridor towards the back of the house.

A moment later, a rather stout woman dressed in a floral printed dress with a plain grey cardigan came up the hallway towards them. The woman appeared to be in her early to mid-fifties, although she could have been younger, with short wavy hair that was shaded somewhere between blonde and grey. She was wearing rather too much makeup.

"Mrs McCranny?" Burke said stepping forward into the hall.

"Yes. How can I help you?"

"Is there somewhere we could have a word?" Burke said.

"Yes, OK, come through," Mrs McCranny said, concern now beginning to appear on her face.

The detectives were shown into a spacious lounge, immaculately presented with a very pale green carpet, two deep cushioned settees, upholstered in a pale green brocade and piped with gold, and an impressive corbelled marble fireplace with shiny brass irons laid out precisely in front of it. A large gilt overmantel mirror reflected the generous velvet drapes that hung on the two casement windows opposite, topped with deep tasselled pelmets. A bow-fronted and highly polished mahogany sideboard standing between the windows, adorned with gleaming silverware of various kinds, completed the furnishings.

"Please, take a seat. Can I arrange some tea or coffee?"

"No thanks. We're fine. Mrs McCranny, may I ask where your husband is today?" Moore said.

"He had a meeting in town. He left early. Why do you ask?"

"Does your husband drive a black BMW, registration number 171-D-265889?" Moore continued.

"Well, he has a black BMW all right, but I don't know the number, I'm afraid. Why, what's all this about?" the woman said.

"Mrs McCranny, I'm very sorry to have to tell you that we came across a black BMW that had been involved in an accident up on the Blessington road earlier this morning. We have reason to believe that your husband was the driver of the car, and I'm sorry to say, he didn't survive," Burke said.

"No, officer, you have that wrong. My husband is attending a meeting in the city. He has offices in Mayor Square on the quays. It must be someone else."

Burke looked uneasily at Moore.

"Have you spoken to your husband since he left home this morning, Mrs McCranny?" Moore said.

"No, of course not. I told you, he's in a meeting."

"I wonder if you would mind calling his mobile now for us?" she went on.

The woman got up and strutted out of the room, unconvinced by what the detectives had told her.

Burke whispered to his colleague, "What now?"

"Let's see what happens with the phone. Then we'll have to tell her about the driving license and credit cards. Shhh, here she comes."

Mrs McCranny came back into the room holding an iPhone in a pink leather case. She sat down on the edge of one of the sofas and dialled a contact from the list. After the phone at the other end rang a few times, Burke and Moore could hear that it had gone to voicemail.

"He must be still in the meeting," the woman said confidently, cancelling the call.

"Mrs McCranny, I think you should know that we retrieved a wallet containing a driver's license and some credit cards from the man who was driving the crashed BMW. They were in the name of Gerald McCranny," Moore said, as sympathetically as she could manage.

"This is ridiculous! Where is the driver of the car now? Take me to him, and I'll prove to you that it is not my husband."

The detectives began to doubt what they had discovered out on the Blessington road themselves. Could they have somehow got it wrong? Could the driver be anyone other than McCranny? They hardly thought so, but it was going to be a tough one convincing the wife without her formally identifying the body, and they weren't ready for that yet.

"Why don't we drive you into town to your husband's offices, Mrs McCranny, and see if we can raise him there?" Moore said.

"Yes, very well. Good idea. I'll just tell Janine that I'm going out, and get my coat."

The woman got up and left the room for a second time.

"Jesus, boss. This is going to be mighty awkward!" Moore said when she had left the room.

"I'll go in my car. You go with her in hers. As soon as I'm on my own, I'll call O'Higgins, and tell him to have McCranny in a fit state to be identified. Then when you can't reach hubby at the office, suggest to the woman that you go around to the morgue. OK?"

"Yeah, I suppose. It's all we can do, really."

Mrs McCranny came back dressed for the outdoors, and agreed to the configuration that Burke had suggested. The two vehicles set off in convoy, and when Burke got back out on the road, he called O'Higgins using the hands-free arrangement in his car.

He explained the plan to the good doctor, and went on to say, "And can you ask the forensic team to give McCranny's car a really good going over. I think there was someone with him, so we need any fingerprints, hair samples, fibres and what have you from the passenger's side."

"Right, Inspector, I'll get them onto it right away. I saw the car going past on the low loader a few minutes ago."

"Thanks, Doc. Moore and the wife should be with you in about thirty to forty minutes."

"OK. I'll be ready for them."

Chapter Three

Burke was back at the office when Moore called him.

"Jesus, boss, that was rough," she said.

"I bet. What happened?"

"Well, he wasn't at the office, obviously, so I asked her to accompany me to the morgue to eliminate the driver, like she said she would. O'Higgins had just about got him tidied up, and of course she identified him as her husband. I was lucky. I got Peggy Ryan, the liaison officer to go back home with her until she can get some family around. She was in bits."

"Why was Peggy in bits?" Burke said.

"Ha ha, very funny. What do you want me to do now?"

"Get back here as soon as you can. I want you to set up a murder room – you know, all the usual palaver."

"OK. See you in a few minutes, but I need to grab something to eat on the way. Want anything brought back?" Moore asked.

"Yeah, OK. Thanks. Just a sambo and a coffee. Cheers."

Burke went to update Superintendent Heffernan while he was waiting for Fiona Moore to get back to the station.

* * *

"OK, so what have we got so far?" Burke asked when they were back in the office together. Moore had set up a whiteboard, and opened a 'Murder Book' on the computer system into which she had input some basic details about the case.

"Well, McCranny wasn't where he was supposed to be, for starters. And I don't think he was alone either," Moore said.

"Right. So, who was he with, and why? Have forensics started work on the car yet? Anything doing?" Burke said.

"They've started, but they won't have anything till around midday tomorrow, or so they say. Oh, and they did recover a mobile phone that looks as if it was McCranny's, but it's locked."

"OK. We'll get the techies onto that. It might hold some information as to why he was where he was. I presume we haven't had any luck trying to find the passenger, if there was one?"

"No. Uniform are still searching the area, but it's heavily wooded and there are just a few houses, so he or she could be anywhere. And I've asked Mrs McCranny to come in tomorrow morning. We need to interview her about her husband – his friends and enemies and so on."

"Right, well you handle that then. I'm going around to his office first thing with a few uniforms – see if we can find out what he was up to in business terms. Let's leave it at that for this evening, then. Let the guys get on with it. What time is Mrs McCranny coming in?" Burke said.

"I suggested twelve o'clock, and she seemed OK with that."

* * *

When they had finished their meeting, Burke left the office, but Moore stayed on a while updating the system and tidying away some papers that had collected during the day while she was out. She hadn't really anything to go home to. However, she was just about to leave when the sergeant who had been in charge of the men searching for the mysterious passenger from McCranny's car called her.

"Hi Fiona, it's Daniel here. We've had a good look around the area where the car went off the road. We've called to any of the houses that are occupied, and scoured the woods in the immediate vicinity with dogs, but there's nothing. How sure are you that there was even a passenger in the car?"

"Hi Daniel. Not sure at all, to be honest. But thanks for having a good look for us. I guess you want to stand the men down at this stage?"

"Yes. It's bloody freezing out here, and it's getting dark now too, so it would be dangerous to continue. I think we'll call it a day."

"Right, so. Thanks for your help anyway."

"You're welcome. Bye."

After the call, Moore locked her PC screen, put on her jacket, scarf and overcoat and went down to the car park to drive home in her Ford Focus. Her home was a rented apartment on the north side of Dublin bordering Marino and Clontarf – the builder had managed to get it classified as the latter, so the value of his properties was enhanced. She was fortunate that it came with a designated parking space, and being a few years old, it was a bit more spacious than the current crop of shoeboxes selling for enormous sums in the coveted Dublin 3 area.

Moore stopped off at the Spar in Fairview and purchased a chilled chicken breast and some ready peeled potatoes that would comprise her evening meal, supplemented by some frozen vegetables she had in the small compartment of her fridge. She still struggled with her weight, but was determined not to let herself get heavy again as she had been as a teenager.

When she had cooked and eaten her dinner, she sat back on the sofa and picked up the Northside News – a free newspaper that dropped into her letterbox once a week.

"Look at me," she said to herself, "I'm a sad bitch! I'll have to get something going for myself. This is daft."

Being late in the year, the paper was populated with advertisements for a generous supply of evening classes that were getting underway. As she perused the paper and scanned the ads for everything from a single session on flower arranging to an accredited degree in any of a host of fairly serious qualifications, an idea came to her.

"Hmm… that could be a bit of gas!" she said, smiling to herself. She clipped a small rectangle out of the paper and put it in her handbag with a view to following it up the next morning.

Chapter Four

Dinny O'Leary's official title was 'Woodland Curator'. At this time of year, most of the work that took place – thinning out the forest and harvesting the tall, straight softwood trees – was over. The giant machines that could fell, strip and chop an entire tree into lorry-friendly lengths in a matter of seconds, had long departed.

For the winter months, Dinny's job involved attempting to keep the rabbits, squirrels and other pests away from the saplings that had been planted during the long summer days, and making the outer perimeter secure. Privately owned vehicles were not permitted in the forested area, except by special arrangement, but stiles were positioned here and there around the fence to facilitate walkers and those who liked to study nature.

At various places throughout the densely wooded terrain, small huts had been positioned that permitted the forestry workers to prepare hot drinks and take their lunch breaks. They were rudimentary structures, built of timber off-cuts from the forest with a corrugated iron roof, usually with a cast iron stove installed, or occasionally a bottled gas cooker with two small burners. All around the huts, both inside and outside, notices warning of the dire consequences of fire were posted, and the huts themselves were located in small, open clearings, in case the worst happened, so that they could burn out without setting the woodland ablaze.

Dinny was working on his own that day, his fellow curator having taken the day off to visit his elderly mother in hospital. He arrived at work before eight o'clock, parking his old green Toyota Corolla van in the deserted car park at the entrance to the woods on the L3160 – a narrow single-track lane that ran around one edge of the plantation, on the opposite side of the forest to where the BMW had been found. Before locking up his car, he put on his well-insulated hi-vis jacket, changed from his driving shoes into his heavy work boots, and tucked the two-litre bottle of clean water that he would use to make tea under his arm. He then left the car, climbed over the fence and trudged off in the direction of the nearest workman's hut. As he made for the shelter of the little building, the smell of damp pine needles and wet moss came to him, as if he needed a reminder that winter had arrived in earnest.

It was getting bright, and a low watery sun began to shine through the trees, creating a patchwork of light and dark on the forest track. Dinny reached the hut, and pushed the wooden door inwards. They had tried locking these small refuges previously, but inevitably the locks were broken off from the thin timber by marauding youths who used the shelters for nefarious purposes during the summer nights. In any case, there was nothing of value to be found there, so the forestry workers had given up trying to secure the places long ago.

It was a lot darker inside the hut than it had been outside, so Dinny didn't immediately see the body lying on the earthen floor, twisted in an unlikely pose and stark naked. But as he turned around, his feet tripped over the bare legs of the man lying on the ground, and he fell backwards, landing on his backside on the rough wooden bench along one wall of the shed.

"Good Jesus!" Dinny exclaimed, as the true nature of the situation dawned on him. His water bottle had fallen to the ground and burst open, so that the contents were pooling around the naked body of the corpse. Dinny scrambled back to his feet and got outside as quickly as he could. His heart was pounding, and his breath short, but he managed to extract his old push-button Nokia phone from his inside pocket, and he called the depot to speak to his manager.

"Christ, Dinny – have you called the Gardaí, or an ambulance?" the man said on hearing the news.

"No, no. I called you first. What will I do?"

"Call 999 as soon as you can. Are you OK? It must have been a terrible shock."

"It was that, for sure. I've never known the like of it. I'm fierce shaken up," Dinny said.

"Well, get on to the police and they'll know what to do. Stay there till they arrive, and don't go back into the hut. Don't touch anything, OK?"

"Yes, sure. I'll wait in my car. God, this is awful. Thanks, Fergus. I'd better call them now."

Dinny's 999 call was routed through to Tallaght Garda station. The officer who took the call made the connection to the earlier crime involving the BMW, and quickly relayed the details of the latest discovery through to Store Street, where Aidan Burke, who had just arrived in to work, was informed.

"Righto. We'll take it from here. But can you get a couple of uniformed officers out to preserve the scene till we get there?" Burke asked.

With the arrangements made, Burke collected Moore from the open plan, and once again they set off in his Volvo for the Dublin Mountains.

* * *

"Do you think there's a connection between the two incidents, boss?" Moore said as they drove out towards the scene.

"What do you think? If there isn't, it's a bloody awful coincidence. And I don't like coincidences, as you know."

"Did you get any information on the casualty?"

"Christ, Fiona, what's with the twenty questions? No, I didn't. The man that found the body is in shock – he could barely speak. What I want to know is how come our lot didn't find this dude yesterday, what with their dogs and everything."

"Apparently, it's at the far side of the plantation. They mustn't have got that far before it fell dark."

The rest of the journey was completed in silence.

Burke pulled his car in beside Dinny's at the entrance to the wood. Dinny was still sitting in his old van, and although he was visibly shaken by what he had found, he was probably over the worst of it. The two young officers that had come out from Tallaght in a squad car had brought coffee with them, and Dinny had been given the hot, sugary drink which no doubt accounted at least in part for his improved condition.

"Morning, men. What's the story?" Burke said to the nearest of the two Gardaí who had got out of their car when they saw Burke approaching.

"We've taped it off. We didn't disturb anything. Looks like the body of a young man. He's naked, and there's something carved into his chest – but we didn't go in, so I can't say what it says," the young Garda reported.

"Right, well, forensics are on their way. But I'd like to have a quick look before they get here. Can you show me where it is?"

"Yes, of course, sir. Follow me."

Before setting off into the undergrowth, Burke instructed Moore to get a statement from Dinny, and then let him away home. He threw her the keys of the Volvo, and then followed the uniformed Garda into the woods.

Burke had donned blue plastic overshoes and blue vinyl gloves as he approached the little building which had been cordoned off with blue and white crime scene tape. He ducked under, and approached the hut, using his torch to peer inside at the body. The corpse was that of a man in his very late teens or early twenties. He was thin, with shoulder-length mousy-coloured hair and a crop of fluff on his chin. He had obviously been stabbed in the neck, and while his heart pumped its last few beats, a quantity of the man's blood had been emitted which lay in a sticky pool around his head.

Burke shone the torch on the man's hairless chest, and saw the letters 'F A G' engraved into the man's skin.

Burke withdrew from the hut and looked all around it, but could see no obvious signs of a presence – no convenient boot prints in the soft moss underfoot; no scraps of cloth snagged on any nearby branches; in fact, no visible evidence of anything much. He decided to leave it to the experts, and headed back to the car park.

* * *

Burke found Moore sitting in the Volvo with the driver's door open.

"Look, there's not much more I can do till the forensic boys have finished up. Is it ok if I leave you here? I want to go and talk to the people in McCranny's office and see what they have to say, and McCranny's wife is coming in at twelve. Can you hitch a lift back to town with some of this lot?" Burke said, gesturing to the several Garda vehicles that had turned up at the scene.

"Yes, OK. I'll see you back later," Moore said. She wasn't too pleased to be left stranded halfway up the Dublin Mountains, but she knew better than to challenge her boss openly, so she said nothing.

Burke got into his car and sped off towards the city.

Chapter Five

McCranny's office was in a recently built block on the corner of Mayor Square, the trendy new area beside the river that had been built after the tenements had been demolished some years ago. The glass door onto the street was locked, but there was a video phone and bell arrangement, and Burke gave it a nice long push.

A moment later, a female voice responded, "I'm sorry, we're closed to the public today."

"Police. I need to come in," Burke said, and a second later a buzzer sounded, allowing him to pull the door towards him and gain entry.

There was an aluminium sign with black writing declaring that reception was on the first floor, and Burke climbed the stairs, entering a generous area with fashionable grey carpet and modern office fittings. The reception desk was positioned between two windows that looked out onto the street, and behind the young, dark-haired girl seated at her PC, Burke observed a frame attached to the wall with several company names listed in the same aluminium with black writing.

The nameplates read in descending sequence, 'McCranny Construction Ltd, McCranny Group Holdings

Ltd, McCranny Commercial Ltd, McCranny Enterprises Ltd, McCranny Homes Ltd', and finally 'McCranny Property Management Ltd'.

"Good morning, my name is Inspector Burke," he said holding out his warrant card, "I'd like to speak to the manager please."

The girl, who was quite pretty, well dressed and nicely turned out replied, "I'm afraid there is no manager, Inspector. There's just me and Sinéad here in the office. All the men are out on site – well, maybe not today – and Mr McCranny looked after all the management stuff."

"I see. And your name is?"

"Melissa. Melissa Brady. I do the phones, the correspondence, the photocopying and the filing, and Sinéad does the books and payments and looks after the accounts."

"Is that it? Just the two of you?"

"Yes, that's it. Mr McCranny did everything else. Of course, we have surveyors, architects and planning consultants in a good lot of the time as well."

"I see. And what projects have you on-going at the moment?"

"It's mostly apartments, though we do have one commercial development in Clondalkin. We're knocking down an old string of shops and rebuilding new ones with offices and apartments overhead. It's nearly finished."

Burke looked at a chair that was over against the wall beside the door where he had come into the room.

"Oh, sorry. Yes, please take a seat. Can I get you a coffee?"

"Yes, please, that would be very nice. Milk, no sugar, thanks."

Melissa disappeared through another door that Burke assumed led to a kitchenette. He took the opportunity to have a good nosey on her desk, but found nothing out of the ordinary – just a few files and a few bills that had been stamped 'Received' with that day's date in red ink on them.

When Melissa returned, she held a mug of coffee and a saucer with two chocolate biscuits that she put down in front of Burke on the edge of her desk.

"Thanks, Melissa. I wonder if you could give me a list of all the developments that you are working on at the moment, and a list of employees too?" Burke said, sampling the coffee which was not at all bad.

"Sure, but we don't really have any employees, except Sinéad and myself. All the building is done by sub-contractors. I can get you a list of those if you like?"

"Yes, OK, but it's not urgent. I can call back. Is the business doing well?"

"I think so. I have only been working here for eleven months, but as far as I can judge it's fine. Sinéad would have a better idea. She's been here for a few years."

"What was McCranny like to work for?" Burke said.

"Fine. We didn't socialise or anything. He kept himself to himself mostly. He was polite, and could be generous at times."

"Oh. How so?"

"Well, he'd sometimes send Sinéad and I out for a long lunch on expenses if things weren't too busy. He'd tell us to go to Jury's Inn, and take our time – have a couple of glasses of wine. That sort of thing."

"Nice. Did you ever meet any of his friends?"

Melissa shot a nervous glance at Burke, and then looked down at her desk.

"No, Inspector."

"Right. Well, I have to go soon. I'd like to have a quick look at Mr McCranny's office before I go though, if that would be OK?"

"Yes, I guess. It's terrible news about the poor man. What happened?" Melissa said, getting up and collecting a key from her desk drawer.

"Too early to say, Melissa. We're just starting the investigation. But I can tell you that his car went off the road up behind Tallaght."

Melissa was walking towards another grey door a little bit down the corridor.

"He was always driving that car of his too fast, poor man," she said. She opened the office door and stood back to let Burke in. At the same time, the telephone rang, and the girl excused herself to go and answer it.

McCranny's office was functional, but tending towards plush. There was a better carpet and an original Victorian or Edwardian mahogany partner's desk with a leather top decorated with gold embossing around the edges, standing at an angle well back from the door. Four period brown leather upholstered dining chairs with ceramic castors were positioned in front of the desk, which had an old captain's chair behind it. A vintage ivory Bakelite, rotary dial telephone sat on the desk alongside a modern device, and a Mont Blanc pen set lay open beside them. A brass lamp with a curved stem and a green glass shade completed the retro look.

The other furniture in the room included a round mahogany pod table – the kind that has a hinged top that can be folded vertically to save space when it's not in use, and a couple of bookcases loaded with technical books on architecture and building, all with matching dark blue leather spines. Adjacent to the old desk, a modern PC stand stood incongruously with a very new looking Apple Mac perched upon it. The distinct smell of stale cigar smoke hung in the air.

Burke nipped around to the business side of the desk and tried the drawers, but they were all locked.

"Don't you need a warrant for that?" A pretty blonde girl dressed in a dark-coloured business suit with her shoulder-length hair tied back in a ponytail stood in the doorway.

"Sinéad, I presume."

"Yes, that's right. I really don't think you should be snooping around like this, Inspector," she said, advancing further into the room.

"I'm sorry for your loss, Sinéad, but as I'm sure you can appreciate, there are some enquiries that must be made at this time. I know Mr McCranny's death looked like a car accident, but there may be more to it, so we need to look into things thoroughly."

"What do you mean?"

"We need to get as much information about your boss as we can, so that we can see what's what. I have to go now, but I'll be back with a colleague tomorrow, and I'd like to have a look over the accounts and stuff with you. I hope that won't be a problem."

"I think I'll ask the firm's solicitor to tag along, Inspector. You won't find anything out of the ordinary here, but all the same."

"That's up to you, Sinéad. Shall we say ten o'clock?"

"Fine."

Sinéad had retreated back into the doorway and was holding the door by the handle, making it quite clear the inspector's visit was over.

* * *

When Burke arrived back to the station shortly before twelve, Mrs McCranny was already waiting in the foyer. She wore a smart camel coat and expensive brown leather gloves, but still had too much make-up on, so that her face was almost orange.

"Good morning, Mrs McCranny, and thanks for coming in. Just give me a minute and then we'll have a chat."

The Garda station had a visitor's room which was sometimes used for discussions with those who were not being officially interrogated. It was always kept clean, and it was informally furnished with a sofa and two easy chairs, although there was also a pale grey table and a couple of office chairs in case things took a more serious tone.

Burke asked the desk sergeant to show the woman in, and they sat down with Mrs McCranny occupying a goodly portion of the sofa while Burke took one of the easy chairs. Mrs McCranny was offered coffee, but declined.

The conversation Burke had with the newly widowed woman revealed very little. It was clear that they led very separate lives, and Mrs McCranny wasn't even sure of her husband's close associates.

"All of Gerald's friends are based around his work, Inspector. We don't socialize together, for obvious reasons, and to be honest, I haven't a clue what he got up to most of the time, and I don't really want to."

"Was your husband in good health, I mean, generally, Mrs McCranny?"

"Yes, as far as I know. He got a good bit of exercise playing golf, and apart from those dreadful cigars, he looked after himself quite well. Why do you ask?"

"I'm sorry if this is a bit indelicate, but when we found him, he had been quite sick. His clothes were covered in it. Did he have any stomach problems?"

"No, as I said, he was in pretty good shape. He may have taken the odd Rennie after a big meal, but he didn't complain about anything like that."

"Was he attending a doctor regularly?"

"He may have had health checks from time to time to do with his insurance, Inspector. I couldn't really say, and before you ask, I don't know who the doctor was. Maybe the office would have a record."

Burke had rarely, if ever, come across a married couple that were quite so independent. He tried several more times to quiz the woman about her husband's lifestyle, but finally he drew the conclusion that the woman simply didn't have any useful information to impart.

Chapter Six

Dr Malcolm O'Higgins was looking down at the body of the young man.

"Cripes, Sergeant, you sure know how to pick them. Not to mention the location. There's no great mystery as to how this one met his end. But we need to scour the area for evidence before we move him back to town," O'Higgins said.

"OK, well, there's no hurry on my part. Any news on the one from the car?" Moore said.

"Not yet. I hardly got a chance to start on him when you called me out to this one. I'll be doing a full PM in the morning though. Fancy coming along?"

"Wild horses, Doc. What time?"

"Let's say ten o'clock. We don't want to disturb your beauty sleep."

"Fat chance. Ok, ten it is. I might bring the inspector along too if he's around."

"Fine. There's no extra charge!"

The doctor went back to his grim work, examining the corpse, taking swabs and photographing the wound in the man's neck and the carving on his torso. His colleagues were searching the hut and the ground around it for any evidence of the perpetrator.

Moore felt that she wasn't adding any value, so she approached one of the uniformed Gardaí who didn't seem to be busy and asked for a lift back to town.

* * *

By the time Moore got to the station, Burke had finished interviewing Mrs McCranny and was sitting at his desk nursing a coffee. The remains of a mostly eaten sandwich was there too, along with the empty wrapper.

"Hi," she said, "how did you get on?"

"You first."

"Not much to tell really, beyond what you saw. O'Higgins is going to do the PM on McCranny tomorrow at ten. Fancy it?"

"I'd love to, but I promised to call back to McCranny's office tomorrow morning, so can you go?" Burke said.

"Yes, sure. How did you get on with the wife?"

"Interesting. It seems they weren't really close. She said they had been using separate bedrooms for the last five years, and she didn't spend a lot of time with her husband. She's pretty heavily into a few charities that keep her busy, so she couldn't tell me what he's been up to at all, really."

"Odd. Have they got kids?" Moore asked.

"Yes. Two boys and a girl. The boys are fully weaned and living away from home. The girl is attending Trinity College and still lives in Foxrock. So, what do you think?"

"You mean is there a connection between the two deaths?"

"Yes. Well, it's a bit of a coincidence, isn't it?" Burke said.

"Let's see what forensics come up with, but a dollar gets you ten there's a link, wait till you see."

"OK. So, what are we doing now, boss?" Moore said.

"I've changed my mind. Let's go back around to McCranny's offices. I said we'd be there in the morning, but the accounts girl said she'd have a solicitor there at that time, so I'd like to catch them unawares. And the girl on the front desk was hiding something – so, see if you can get her to open up while I'm busy with the good-looking blonde."

"Some things never change – typical! C'mon, let's go," Moore said, smiling.

* * *

"We weren't expecting you till the morning," Melissa said when Burke and Moore entered the reception area.

"I know," Burke replied, "but we just need to check out a few things. Is Sinéad in her office?"

"Yes. I'll let her know you're here."

"No, it's OK, I'll just go straight in," Burke said heading for the door.

Without further ado, Burke marched into the girl's office.

"Oh, Inspector – we weren't expecting you back today. What can I do for you?"

"Hello, Sinéad. I'd like to see some recent bank statements for the main operating companies, if that's OK?"

"Don't you need a warrant or something? Anyway, why would that be of interest? Poor Mr McCranny died in a car crash, didn't he?" Sinéad said.

Sinéad was a gorgeous-looking girl, and her outfit showed off her figure so that Burke had to check himself to avoid getting distracted.

"Look, Sinéad, I'm not sure that it was entirely an accident. There are complications that I can't go into just yet, but it's important that we know what the state of the companies is. If I have to get a warrant, the whole place will be crawling with uniformed Gardaí, and it can be very disruptive. Best if we do it here and now one to one."

Sinéad thought for a moment and then said, "How do you mean about the accident. He just drove into a tree, didn't he?"

"Maybe. But it's not quite as simple as that, so we're digging a little deeper. Can I see the most recent bank statements?"

Sinéad flipped through a small pile of papers on her desk, and pulled out two sheets stapled together.

"Here you go. This is for the main company. The others don't really do much."

Burke studied the statement, seeing that there was a healthy balance in the account. The payments out seemed to be to other building firms, and he could see the women's wages listed too.

"You're both pretty well paid. Are his taxes up to date?"

"Yes. We are nearly always in a VAT reclaim position because of the nature of the work. But the income tax is all in order. Would you like to see?"

"No, that's fine. I'll take your word for it," Burke said, smiling broadly at the girl.

"Did Mr McCranny draw a salary?"

"Yes, he did. €150,000 before you ask. And his wife did too. She's a director, but hers was only €50,000."

"Nice. I presume the company could afford it?"

"Yes, of course. As you can see, we're very solvent."

"What about the other companies? There seems to be quite a long list pinned to the wall out in reception."

"As I said, Inspector, they don't really do much. We just use them at various times when the occasion demands."

"Right, well thanks for letting me see these. I may have to come back again at some stage. What will you do about keeping the place open?"

"I don't know. I think Mrs McCranny is going to make some arrangements, but I don't know what they are just yet. I hope she doesn't close us down, but with Gerry gone

– well, you know, he was the driving force behind the business."

"OK. Well, I hope it works out for you anyway," Burke said.

"Thanks, I'm sure we'll be fine."

Burke got up and went back out to the reception area where Moore was just finished chatting to Melissa. They left, and when they were back in the car, Burke asked Moore how she had got on.

"She didn't say too much, but there's something she's not telling me. I asked if McCranny ever tried it on with either of them, and she went all shy and looked away. But she didn't say anything."

"Do you think he was at her?"

"No. She's not upset enough for that. But there's something amiss. It will come out sooner or later. How did you get on with blondie?"

"Pretty good. She wasn't nearly as frosty as she had been earlier. The accounts look to be in good shape. The place is making good money. But she's not sure what will happen now. There's no obvious successor. Oh, and she gave me a list of the projects that McCranny has been working on for the last year or so. She also called him 'Gerry' at one stage, so maybe there was something there, I dunno. You couldn't blame him. When we get back, can you get the boys to start doing background checks on them? Get onto the Companies Office website and download the accounts for all of the firms listed in the hallway, and get the directors and anything else relevant while you're at it."

"Yes, OK. What are we looking for?"

"Just anything that looks a bit off – you know – planning permissions, contract values that could be excessive; that sort of thing," Burke said.

"God, we'll need some expert help with that, unless you have some hidden talents I don't know about."

"I don't. Get some help from the Office of Public Works. They'll have architects and surveyors sitting on their arses over there who will enjoy a bit of a diversion."

"Right. Let's get back and see what forensics have got. They should have an ID on the young guy by now at least," Moore said.

Chapter Seven

When Moore got back to her desk, there was a message for her to call Dr O'Higgins. She dialled his number.

"Dr O'Higgins, it's Fiona Moore."

"Hello, Sergeant. Thanks for calling back. I thought you might like to have some of the preliminaries from the McCranny thing."

"Oh, yes please, what have you got?"

"Quite a lot really. Are you sitting down?"

"Go on."

"Firstly, the car crash wasn't what killed the man. It may have knocked him out, but it's not what he died from. It was far less severe than it looked," Dr O'Higgins said.

"So, what did kill him?"

"I don't know yet. We'll find out in the morning when I have the toxicology results back."

"I see. Anything else?" Moore said.

"Yes. The car. The lads are still working on it, but so far, they've found a lot of semen on the seats – both front seats – and on the floor mats. We're doing tests now to see if there's a match with McCranny."

"Hmm. Can you test to see if any of it matches the lad we found in the woods too?"

"Yes, of course, naturally."

"Any sign of other bodily fluids – from a woman, say?"

"No. Nothing like that."

"When will you have the results of the match?"

"Possibly later on this evening. I'll give you a call when we have something."

"OK. Thanks, Doc. Any ID on the young lad yet?"

"Maybe. Some of your lot think it might be one Felix Lahart. He probably has form. I'll run his prints just as soon as I get a minute – see if he's known to us," the doctor said, sighing.

"Thanks. We'll wait to hear from you."

Moore went into Burke's office and brought him up to speed on her conversation with the doctor.

"Hmm. Interesting. What do you make of it?"

"It's obviously not straightforward. But if McCranny was into some sort of kinky sex, it could explain why the missus has removed herself from his bed."

"Yes, that makes sense. Well, we'll have the cause of death in the morning. Now we have to figure out why," Burke said.

"Right, there's not a lot more we can do here till the morning. Fancy an early bird?" he went on.

Moore was a bit taken aback by the unexpected invitation, but did her best not to show it.

"Yes, OK. What do you feel like?"

Burke hesitated a moment and smirked before replying.

"Italian?"

"Great. Give me a few minutes to get ready."

* * *

They were seated near the back of Trattoria di Pescara just off O'Connell Street. It was one of the oldest Italian restaurants in Dublin, and still boasted white table linen, good cutlery, and genuine Italian waiters. There were small electric lamps on the tables each with a red fabric shade that lent a cosy, intimate atmosphere to the place.

The waiter, immaculately dressed in black pants, a starched white shirt and a bow tie presented them with an oversized menu apiece.

"Red or white?" Burke said as Moore opened the menu and started to study it.

"Not so fast, tiger. I haven't looked at the wines yet."

They ordered the antipasti, to be followed by lasagne with a side salad, and Moore chose a bottle of Campofiorin to accompany the meal.

A few minutes later the waiter brought a magnificent plate of mixed seasoned meats with some white asparagus on the side and a basket of crusty ciabatta bread. Another waiter produced the wine, making a great show of presenting the bottle to Burke so that he could inspect the label. When it was opened, Burke indicated that Moore should do the tasting, and her nod of approval allowed the waiter to pour half a glass each for them.

As they set about the starters, Moore asked, "So, Aidan, any more thoughts of retirement?"

Moore had previously found a partially completed application form on Burke's desk that would have seen him leave the force on full pension as soon as he reached fifty years of age, if it had been submitted to the superintendent.

Burke avoided eye contact, busying himself with the food.

"It's on hold for the moment," he said.

"I should hope so too. And how are you getting on with everything yourself?"

"Ah, ye know."

"No, I don't know. That's why I asked," Moore said.

"I'm OK. I've cut back a lot on the booze, and I got the house fixed up. I have that cleaning company coming in once a fortnight to keep it nice. And I got a new kitchen, like you suggested."

"Cool. Bet that feels better."

"Yeah, it does. A lot better. I'm thinking of taking a lodger to help with the mortgage. Deirdre is squeezing me dry, as usual, and I'm sure I could get a fresh-faced young Garda just up from the country to take a room. Renting is so bloody dear now in the city, I'd probably get five or six hundred a month for the spare room."

"Would that not cramp your style a bit?" Moore said.

"Style – what style? Oh, you mean the constant stream of gorgeous young women that I have coming back to the house every night? Get real, Sergeant. Been there – done that – got the T-shirt. No more! Anyway, what about you?"

"What about me?" Moore said.

"Where's your love life at?"

Just then the waiter returned and removed their very clean plates, providing a welcome diversion while Moore composed her response. Another waiter placed a dish of bubbling lasagne down before each of them, and offered each a sprinkling of freshly grated Parmesan cheese.

"Some detective you are." She paused for a moment. "Ground zero, Aidan. Nada."

"God, we're a sorry pair. But I thought you might have snagged an eager young Garda by now, Fiona."

"Have you seen what's actually on offer? And I'm very, very fussy!"

"Clearly," Burke said, and the two tucked into the delicious meal.

Chapter Eight

The two detectives arrived into the station at almost the same time the following morning, but not together. After the meal the previous night, they had been for a drink in The Bank on College Green, but then had gone their separate ways.

"Will you see if there's anything in from forensics, and then could you get over to the PM? I'm going to have another word with McCranny's wife. We need to know a lot more about Gerald McCranny's social life!" Burke said.

"Yes, OK. Catch up later," Moore said.

She went to her desk in the open plan office, and logged into her PC. There was indeed a report in from forensics, and it made interesting reading. Firstly, they had been able to match some of the semen found on the floor of McCranny's car with that of the young man found dead in the workman's hut. Secondly, Dr O'Higgins had opined, formally, that McCranny's cause of death was not the car accident. The second useful piece of information was that the carving in the youth's torso was not done with the same instrument that was used to stab him to death. The word 'FAG' had been sliced into his skin using something very rough and jagged, and those wounds had been inflicted after he was dead.

There had been no trace of a weapon found near the body, or in the vicinity of the old hut, and the terrain was not conducive to capturing footprints.

Moore printed off the report from her PC, put it in a manila folder and left it on Burke's desk before setting off to the post-mortem.

* * *

Burke had called ahead to make sure that Mrs McCranny would be at home at ten o'clock. When he arrived, he rang the bell and was greeted by the same young girl that they had met before. She showed him into the sitting room, which smelled of fresh furniture polish, and was still in immaculate order. After a couple of minutes, Mrs McCranny came into the room, looking rather haggard.

"Good morning, Inspector. Have you been offered a cup of tea, or coffee?"

"No, it's fine, Mrs McCranny. I won't keep you long."

"Well, sit down at least, Inspector. How can I help you today?" the woman said, as she plonked her rather corpulent frame into one of the easy chairs.

"We were wondering what you know of your husband's businesses."

"Not a lot. Of course, I knew he was a property developer, and I think I'm down as a director. Gerald used to ask me to sign various papers from time to time."

"Did you read the documents before you signed them?"

"No. They wouldn't mean anything to me anyway. I'm not a business person, Inspector."

"What about Mr McCranny's circle of friends. Did you socialise together often?"

"Not often. He had his cronies at the golf club. I'm not a clubby type at all. Of course, we went out to dinner together from time to time, and then there were family gatherings, but generally Gerald mixed in his own circles, and I in mine. We are – were – both very busy people."

"Did Gerald have any friends he was particularly close to?"

"Well, there a Michael Dunne that he played golf with on most Saturdays when the weather allowed. And then there's David Gilchrist – he's another member of the golf club. And Freddy Taylor of course, the architect. Gerald worked very closely with Freddy, and he came to the house quite often, but it was mostly business, I think."

Burke was making notes in his pocketbook as the dead man's wife reeled off the names of his close associates.

"Thanks, Mrs McCranny, that's very helpful. May I ask you about the girls in the office, Melissa and Sinéad I think their names are?"

"What about them?" Mrs McCranny said.

"Well – I'm sorry, this is a bit delicate – but Sinéad in particular is very attractive."

The woman threw her head back and laughed out loud.

"Really, Inspector, haven't you figured it out yet? Gerald was on the other bus!"

Burke shuffled uncomfortably in his seat.

"Sorry, are you saying Mr McCranny was gay?"

"Yes. Exactly. So, I don't think you need worry about Sinéad, Inspector. As far as I know, he didn't swing both ways!"

Burke was taken aback by what the woman had said. After all, from the outside it looked like the McCranny family was a typical nuclear arrangement. But then as Burke's mother had often said to him, 'you never know what's going on behind closed doors'.

"I see. And are you familiar with any of his male friends at all, Mrs McCranny?"

"Oh, good Lord, no. Once he came out to me, as it were, it was game over. I don't know, and I don't want to know about that side of his life, Inspector."

"So, it wasn't generally known that your husband was, eh, well – you know," Burke said.

"Certainly not. It's no one else's business," Mrs McCranny said defiantly.

"What about your children? Are they aware?"

"I think Emily may be. We haven't discussed it, but kids are pretty smart these days, wouldn't you agree? Nothing specific has been said, but I noticed Emily looking at him a bit quizzically a few times lately. To be honest, I can't imagine how you broach that particular subject with your kids."

"Yes, I can see what you mean. So, what will happen with the firm now?"

"I haven't a clue, Inspector. For God's sake, my husband has just died. We'll figure something out in due course. When can I arrange the funeral?"

"I'll let you know on that one. It won't be for a week or two. We need to investigate this whole thing very carefully. I presume you know there was another body found near the scene of your husband's accident?"

"Yes, I saw that on the news. Is there a connection?"

"Well, based on what you've just told me, there may well be. We'll know more in a day or two. Did you husband leave a will, Mrs McCranny?" Burke said.

"Yes. And as far as I know everything will come to me. We had that agreement – we willed everything to each other. I have independent means, you see."

"I see. I wonder if I could get a look at your husband's bank statements – you know, for his personal account? It might help us to identify someone of interest."

"Well, I don't see how. But all that paperwork is kept at the office in any case. You can ask your friend Sinéad for it."

Burke realised that he wasn't going to get anything more of value from the woman, so he thanked her for her time, and left.

* * *

Sergeant Fiona Moore was no fan of post-mortems. She didn't get sick as the procedure was carried out – she had got over that particular embarrassment after the first one she had attended as a rookie – but she would have preferred not to have gone to it.

Dr O'Higgins, dressed in a green rubber splash-proof apron and a blue hat to keep his hair out of the proceedings, hovered over the cadaver looking a tad menacing.

"Good morning, Sergeant, we're just getting started here. Oh, by the way, we found some interesting things when we removed his clothing," the doctor said, arranging his various tools on the trolley adjacent to the gurney on which Gerald McCranny's body was lying.

"What did you find?" Moore disliked the way the pathologist made her ask, as if he held the secret to some complex mystery, and wanted to make the most of its disclosure.

"My assistant here," O'Higgins said, gesturing to a young man dressed in a blue surgical suit who looked about seventeen to Moore, "found pine needles in his shoes. Just a few that had snagged on his socks."

"Are they from the area where the car was found?"

"We'll have to go back and collect some from that wood for comparison, but they could be. There was also a good deal of mud on his shoes, so we'll be matching that up too."

"Well, that's hardly a surprise, Doctor, he was a builder after all. He probably spent a good deal of time on building sites and the like," Moore said.

"This isn't that kind of mud, Sergeant. This is rural mud. Building sites have a particular mixture of fine rubble and cement in the mud. This is purely organic matter, and besides, he had a pair of wellingtons in the boot of the car that he obviously used when he was on site, along with loads of other builder's paraphernalia."

O'Higgins attached a powerful LED lamp to his head, and started on McCranny by slicing the man open in the conventional 'Y' pattern, before reaching in and detaching the man's organs which were placed in stainless steel dishes and ushered away by the young assistant to be weighed.

"So, what did he die of, Doctor?" Moore asked as the dismemberment continued.

This time the good doctor responded almost instantly.

"If I'm not very much mistaken, I'd say he was poisoned."

"Poisoned! Jesus, are you serious?"

"Never more so, Sergeant. I thought that might have been the case when he came in, but what I'm seeing now is leading me to that conclusion."

"What exactly are you seeing, Doctor?"

"Evidence of tachycardia. Some discolouration of the kidneys, and dark red lividity generally. I'm having the blood and urine analysed now for toxins. It won't take long," he said, in a very matter-of-fact manner.

"What kind of poison, Doctor?" Moore said.

"Patience, dear Sergeant, patience. Why don't you go and get yourself a nice hot coffee, and when you get back, I should have some news for you."

Moore left the mortuary and called Burke on her phone, but it went straight to voicemail. She didn't leave a message.

When she was seated in the Starbucks close to the morgue, nursing a cappuccino as prescribed by Dr O'Higgins, her phone rang.

"Moore."

"Ah, hello Sergeant. It's Dr O'Higgins. I said I'd get back to you when we had identified the poison used on your builder friend. Arsenic, and plenty of it. The cigar in the ash tray of the car was full of it, as was his blood. Almost certainly white powder arsenic dissolved in water."

"I see. Any idea of its origin, Doctor?"

"No, not a clue. It's impossible to trace that kind of information, and you'd be surprised just how much of it there is round and about."

"OK. Well thanks, Doc. I'll pass it on."

Chapter Nine

Two hours later, Moore was back at the station and went to find Burke who was ruminating in his office.

"Hi. What's up?" she said.

"Pity I didn't see the folder you left for me before I went to see Mrs McCranny. Made me look a right eejit," Burke said rather crossly.

"Oh. How come?"

"Well, I would have known that our victim was gay, wouldn't I?"

Moore laughed.

"Oh, yes. I bet you got a surprise when that was revealed. I presume the missus told you?" Moore said.

"Yes, she did. Anyway, what have you got?"

"Wait till you hear this. Yer man was only poisoned, wasn't he? The damage from the accident was just superficial. He actually died from arsenic poisoning," Moore said.

"Christ!"

"Exactly. The doctor said it was probably administered via those cigars he smoked. The one from the ashtray in the car was laced with the stuff," Moore said.

"And the doc is sure, is he?"

"Yes, he said the dose was way more than what occurs naturally. He's doing a report, but he's sure that the cigar was injected with a big dose of it. Clever, eh?"

"Maybe. Anything else?"

Moore told Burke about the pine needles and the mud on McCranny's shoes.

"So, what next?" she asked.

"This is nuts. I'm gonna send Dónal out to Tallaght – see if we can find out anything about the other victim. I want to organise a proper search of that wood too. We need to find the young guy's clothes, and whatever weapon was used to kill him. That'll give the uniforms out there something to do. I want you to trawl through McCranny's company data, you know all that stuff we downloaded from the CRO. And set up a briefing for five o'clock. We're going to need some help with this."

"OK. I'll see you later."

* * *

Moore got herself a sandwich and a takeaway carton of soup from the deli across the road and then settled down at her desk to scrutinize the mound of documents that had been downloaded from the Companies Office website.

She was getting heartily fed up after two hours of pouring over years of accounts that looked perfectly normal to her eyes, when she got to the last company on the list – McCranny Property Management Limited. The first thing that she noticed was that Sinéad Walsh was a director of the company. Secondly, this particular business had a very substantial turnover – close to two million euro in the last year, which was contrary to the information that had been provided.

She decided to go back onto the website and download the detailed accounts for that particular company. She printed off almost thirty pages of figures, and set about analysing them with a red pen. Moore was good at this sort of thing. As a Leaving Certificate student, she had done the bookkeeping for her uncle's firm, and made a better job of it than his accountant, or so he said. She enjoyed working with figures, and it wasn't long before she had some very interesting summaries written down on her jotter.

* * *

The afternoon briefing got underway as soon as Burke got back to the station.

"OK, you first, Fiona – what have you got?" he said.

"Right. Well, firstly the girl in McCranny's office was lying to us. Sinéad Walsh is a director of one of the companies, and it has a very significant turnover," Moore said.

"Oh. Which one?" Burke said.

"The maintenance company. Turned over nearly two million last year, and I can't make head nor tail of the individual transactions. You'd expect a lot of small payments in and out for keeping properties running smoothly, but this is different. Almost no money going out at all, except a hefty salary to Little Miss Perfect, and lots of sizeable inpayments, mostly from overseas," Moore said.

"I see. Where did they come from – the inpayments?" Dónal asked.

"I haven't got that far yet, but they're not local, that's for sure. I'll get to work tracing them tomorrow. Now what did you two get out in Tallaght?"

"We've identified the young lad that was found in the hut. One of the local Gardaí recognised him. His name is Felix Lahart, known locally as 'Feely', for obvious reasons. He has quite a back story apparently. From a good family on the southside originally, but dropped out of school at fifteen and got mixed up with a bad lot. He left home, and had been couch-surfing and sleeping rough. Looks like he might have been a rent boy too. Has a few petty crimes logged against him – shoplifting, a bit of drug stuff –

nothing heavy, and one taking and driving away. O'Higgins confirmed the fingerprints against the database, so it's definitely him."

"But no further on with who might have killed him?" Moore said.

"No, I'm afraid not. But it's early days," Burke said.

"OK, so plans for tomorrow. Dónal, can you get back out to Tallaght? Hook up with some of the local Gardaí and mix it up with the low life in the area. Find out if Felix has upset anyone recently, or been in a serious argument. Get the word on the street as it were – you know the drill. And find out if there's anyone in particular that doesn't like gays in the area. It might be worthwhile having a chat with them. Give us a call if you come up with anything. Oh, and you'd better see if we have a contact for Lahart's family. They might just want to be informed!"

"Right, boss, will do," Dónal said.

"Fiona, can you go out to McCranny's house and collect his cigars. Don't say anything about why we want them, just get the wife to hand them over – if it's not too late already. See if you can have a snoop in the bathroom cupboard too. You'd be surprised how often poisoners keep their potions there. But don't get caught."

"OK, boss. Do you think it was the wife?" Moore said.

"I don't think anything until we get some actual evidence, Sergeant. But it's certainly possible, wouldn't you say?"

Moore didn't respond, so Burke went on.

"And when you've done that, will you keep working on McCranny's enterprises? I have a meeting with the Super that will take a couple of hours early on, so we can get together at lunchtime and see what you've found. And everyone, make sure that PULSE is up to date, will you. There's a rumour going around that we're going to be audited at some stage. OK, that's it." Burke got up, signalling the meeting was over.

As he was leaving to go back to his office, Moore said, "A word, boss?"

"Yes, sure. In my office."

When the two were enclosed in his office, Burke said, "So, what's on your mind?"

"Have you got a problem with me, boss?" she said.

"No, 'course not, why?"

"It's just that you keep knocking me back, and just now, in front of colleagues. Just wondering what I've done – or not done?" Moore said.

"Ah, away with ye. There's nothing like that. You're just being too sensitive, girl. You know what I'm like."

"Are you sure there's nothing else?"

"Sure, what else could there be? Look, I'm not going to apologise. I am who I am, like it or leave it, but I'll try to be a bit more careful. How about that?"

"Hmmm… I'm not completely convinced. But at least you didn't ask me if it was my time of the month!"

"None of my business. OK, are we done?"

"Yes, thanks for listening to me."

She felt embarrassed. She was sure they were going to have a more meaningful discussion, but clearly, it was not to be.

"Right, so, see you tomorrow."

Chapter Ten

Moore decided not to go straight home. She went back to her desk and collected the list of properties that McCranny had been developing. A couple of them were in the city centre, and she decided to go and see for herself what sort of properties they were.

The first one she found was an office block on Dawson Street. Since time immemorial, Dawson Street had always played second fiddle to its parallel neighbour, Grafton Street. But since the Luas – Dublin's new tram service – had been put down the street, Dawson Street had acquired an improved status. Several excellent restaurants had made it their home, and the old 1970s office blocks were being torn down and replaced with new ones.

Moore was initially curious as to why relatively new buildings were being demolished in this way. She had discovered that they were largely built of concrete, and the ceiling height was insufficient to accommodate the false floors required by modern IT, and air conditioning ducts that needed to go into the ceiling space. So down they came, to be replaced by more offices that Moore hoped would last a bit longer than fifty years.

In the early winter evening, work had stopped on the building, but a huge skeleton of steel girders, surrounded by a painted hoarding, bearing the name 'Dawson Plaza, a McCranny Development' in enormous navy letters on a grey background was wrapped around the perimeter.

Moore parked her car on Molesworth Street and got out. She took her mobile phone and photographed the site from several angles. She snapped the noticeboard that listed the sub-contractors involved in the construction, and observed that Frederick Taylor & Co, RIAI were listed as the architects for the project.

Moore drove on to the second property on the list. This was an old deserted warehouse on the edge of Dublin port. A rusty chain-link fence, leaning over perilously in places, was all that protected the old red brick building that was still standing, presumably awaiting final planning permission and the bulldozers in that order. The walls were daubed with graffiti, and at one end of the long, narrow construction several slates were missing, exposing dark wooden rafters that had long since succumbed to the rain. The building was surrounded by what had once been a concrete apron, but was now broken and uneven with buddleia growing up between the gaping cracks. A single electric light attached to the corner of the building cast eerie shadows on the yard.

Moore was about to get out of her car when two men came strolling down the street towards the building. They couldn't see her in the darkness, so she waited to observe where they would go. Both where fairly short, dressed in workmen's clothes, and while she couldn't see them too clearly in the gloom, she recognised the swarthy appearance of their skin, which she concluded, put their origin somewhere to the east – possibly Romania, Hungary or even Turkey.

Much to her surprise, the two men prised open the fragile rusty gates and went into the yard. They walked down along the side of the old building, around the corner and disappeared. Moore didn't know what to do. Should she get out and try to find out where they had gone? Should she call for some assistance to explore the building.

"No," she said to herself, "I'm probably being paranoid." But even as she said the words, she realised that it was at least suspicious. The far side of the old shed faced directly onto the water's edge, so if the two men hadn't gone for a swim, they must be inside the building. She waited in the car. There could be more men coming along, after all, and she didn't want to get caught between two lots of them. A minute later, she saw a dull light coming from one of the filthy windows on the second floor.

Moore stayed on for a while, happy that she was more or less invisible to anyone passing by. For the next forty minutes, a steady stream of men came down the road and disappeared into the old wrecked building. She counted twenty-two in all, and they seemed to be similar in appearance. At one stage she quietly wound down her car window, and she could hear a few of them conversing in a language she didn't recognise. By seven o'clock, the arrivals had thinned out, and when she was sure that she wasn't being observed, she took out her phone, disabled the flash function on the camera, and photographed the place.

She moved on to another few of the properties on the list, but found nothing untoward. There was a small mixed development in Sandymount, which was almost finished, the hoarding having been removed and an auctioneer's signboard erected offering fully fitted offices and apartments to rent, with a photograph of the finished block looking rather smarter than the actual place itself. On South Lotts Road there was a string of small cottages that were being renovated and extended, where again wooden panels surrounded the works bearing the name McCranny, and another listing for Frederick Taylor & Co, RIAI.

The other sites were well out of town, so Moore decided that she'd seen enough. She went home.

* * *

The following morning Moore decided to drive directly out to Foxrock to see Mrs McCranny and collect her husband's cigars. She hadn't called ahead, as she didn't want Mrs McCranny to have any chance to destroy them, in case she was in fact implicated in the man's death. The traffic was almost all going the other way, and she was easily able to keep her speed up to the 60 kph limit once she had passed Donnybrook Church.

She arrived at the property at just after a quarter past nine and rang the bell. The same young girl that they had met earlier answered the door.

"Hi. I've come to see Mrs McCranny. I presume she is in?" Moore said.

"Yes, but she's still in bed. She usually rises at ten o'clock when I have her bath ready."

"Well, if you don't mind, I'd like you to get her up. I need to talk to her."

The girl scowled at Moore, no doubt wondering what kind of reception she would get from her employer, before turning back into the house and climbing the stairs. She hadn't said anything more to Moore, and she hadn't invited her in.

Moore waited patiently on the doorstep, and after several minutes spent admiring the manicured gardens and just soaking in the peace of the place, Mrs McCranny finally appeared.

"Good morning, officer. Is this really necessary?" she said crossly. Mrs McCranny was dressed in a lightweight dressing gown with a pale, floral pattern that was tied tightly around her waist emphasising her substantial girth. She wore a pair of fluffy pink slippers, and her hair was bedraggled. Without makeup, the woman looked anything but elegant in the harsh morning light.

"Sorry to disturb you, Mrs McCranny, may I come in?"

"If you must. What is it this time?" Mrs McCranny said, turning and making her way back to the beautiful sitting room with Moore in tow.

Moore didn't reply immediately – not until they were inside the room and they had taken a seat on opposing sofas.

"I'm here to collect Mr McCranny's cigars. We need them for some technical analysis," Moore said.

"Well, you've had a wasted journey, I'm afraid. Gerald didn't keep those smelly things at the house. He must have had them in the office. I couldn't stand the stink they made, although he did insist on smoking them indoors if he happened to have one going when he came home."

The woman stood up, clearly signalling that their short meeting was concluded.

Moore decided that it was pointless trying to get to the bathroom, as Burke had suggested. There was almost certainly a guest bathroom on the ground floor, but that wouldn't have any material evidence to yield in any case. Moore apologised for the intrusion, and left.

She decided to go directly to McCranny's office to see if she could retrieve the man's cigars from there. She didn't want to question Sinéad Walsh without Burke being present, so she wouldn't mention what she had discovered about the property management company just yet.

Moore arrived at the office just before ten o'clock, and found Melissa at the reception desk tapping away on her computer.

"Good morning, Melissa. I wonder if I could collect Mr McCranny's box of cigars please? We need them for some technical analysis back at the station," Moore said.

"Oh, right. I think they're in his desk drawer. Hold on there a moment and I'll go and get them."

Melissa disappeared into McCranny's office, and Moore could hear her talking to a man. She reappeared a few moments later carrying a wooden box of Havana cigars, and offered them to the detective.

"Is there someone in Mr McCranny's office, Melissa?" Moore said.

"Yes. That's Mr Taylor. Mrs McCranny has asked him to step in temporarily while we get things sorted out. There's an awful lot going on that Sinéad and myself just can't handle."

"I wonder if I could have a word with him?"

"Sure, but he's very busy," the girl said, moving back towards what had been Gerald McCranny's office with Moore following.

"Freddy, this is Sergeant Moore. She's investigating Mr McCranny's death," Melissa said.

Taylor was a very handsome man in his late forties or early fifties. He was tall, slim, and had a fine mop of dark hair starting to go grey here and there, which was immaculately cut. He wore a dark grey suit and a pale blue button-down Ralph Lauren shirt that had been lovingly ironed not long ago, and a striped silk tie with some sort of small logo embroidered into it.

Moore extended her hand, and Taylor shook it with a firm, dry grip.

They both started to speak at the same time, but Moore quickly shut up and allowed the architect to continue.

"Pleased to meet you, Sergeant. I'm sorry it's not in more cheerful circumstances."

"Yes, likewise, Mr Taylor. I'm sorry for your loss. It must have come as a terrible shock to you."

"Yes, yes of course."

Moore stayed quiet, and it was obvious that she expected the man to say more, so after a short pause, he went on, "Elizabeth – Mrs McCranny – asked me to come in and see if I could keep the place going for a few weeks till she can make more permanent arrangements. It's handy anyway. Most of my work of late has been for Gerald."

"Yes. I've seen your name on several of the billboards outside Mr McCranny's various developments. Do you have other clients too?"

"Oh, yes. But not as big as McCranny. I have three more partners in the practice, and they generally look after our other clients," Taylor said.

"Can I ask you about that old warehouse down by the river. What's the story there?" Moore said.

"We're waiting for planning permission for that one. It's been quite difficult. There's a group of nearby residents that want it preserved – heaven knows why – it's a dump. But there have been a lot of objections, and it takes ages to work through them. Anyway, hopefully it will be cleared up in the next couple of months, and then we can get going. That is if that's what Elizabeth wants. Look, is there anything else, Sergeant? It's just that I'm rather busy."

"No. Nothing more, for now at least. Sorry to have disturbed you."

Once outside, Moore slipped the box of cigars into a plastic evidence bag. She would drop them off at the technical bureau on her way back to the station.

Chapter Eleven

Detective Garda Dónal Lawler was from a very different background to either Aidan Burke or Fiona Moore. While they had spent their entire time in the force based in Dublin, Dónal had started his career in Waterford, close to where his family came from. He had been a uniformed officer for four years in Waterford City. Then he spent a short spell, still in uniform, in Kilkenny, but when he decided he wanted to be a detective, the only vacancy he could find was attached to Store Street in the centre of Dublin. After two years working with Burke, he reflected that it was no coincidence that that particular post had remained unfilled for some time.

Lawler wasn't as hardened, nor as streetwise as his colleagues. His rural background had given him a gentler introduction to policing, and although he had encountered some quite challenging situations, they were nothing as brutal or as seemingly senseless as this one.

He had found the address for Dr Terence Lahart quite easily. The man was a consultant oncologist. He was attached to the Blackrock Clinic and St Vincent's University Hospital, and had his home in Dalkey – a fashionable and expensive seaside village on the south side of the city.

Lawler decided to try his home address first. Lahart's property was a fine Victorian terraced house overlooking the sea down by Colliemore Harbour. There were granite steps up to the front door, which was painted a subdued navy colour, and expensive looking drapes could be seen adorning the windows on either side of the entrance, tied back with swags.

Lawler parked up, went to the front door and pressed the bell. After a few minutes, which he spent looking out to Dalkey Island and enjoying the sea air, the door was opened a fraction, a security chain preventing it from opening further. Lawler could see the face of a very old woman peeking out, who said in a faint voice, "Yes, what do you want?"

Lawler produced his warrant card and told the old woman that he was hoping to speak to Dr Terence Lahart. Without a word, the door closed momentarily, the chain was released, and finally it opened sufficiently to admit the detective who followed the woman into the front room.

"Terence is in his study. I'll see if he can be disturbed," the woman said, shuffling out of the room a little unsteadily.

Lawler turned his attention to the window which looked out over the harbour. He could see a small cuddy boat in the sound between the land and Dalkey Island lifting pots that the fisherman no doubt hoped would contain a lobster, or at worst a handful of prawns.

Terence Lahart came into the room. He had the confident air of a senior medical man used to ushering nervous students around the wards and intimidating patients with his vast knowledge of whatever ailment they had presented.

"Good morning, Detective, how can I help you?"

"Good morning, Doctor. I was just admiring this beautiful view. It's quite spectacular. May I ask if you have a son called Felix?"

"Oh, Felix," the man said, smiling broadly, "what's he done now?"

"What age would Felix be, Doctor?"

"Let me see, eh, twenty-two, I think. Yes, that's right, twenty-two this year. Why do you ask?"

"And does he live at home with you?"

"Oh, dear God, no. Felix hasn't lived here since he was fifteen." Dr Lahart, seeing the somewhat puzzled look on Lawler's face, decided some form of explanation was required. He went on, "Felix is a troubled boy, Detective. He has a lot of issues. He ran away when he was fifteen. My wife and I were separating at the time, and Felix took it very badly. But that's not all. He got in with a bad crowd." The man sat down and gestured to Lawler to do the same.

"I tried to do what I could, but with the separation going through, and my work – well, you know. It wasn't easy."

"Yes, I'm sure. When did you last see Felix, Doctor?"

"I haven't. Not for more than three years at least. We're not in touch."

"I see, Dr Lahart. I'm sorry to tell you, but we have reason to believe that Felix may have been killed. His body was discovered a few days ago in the woods up behind Tallaght."

"Good heavens. Are you sure it's him?"

"Fairly certain. We will need some final identification, but his fingerprints were on record, and they match Felix."

Lawler said nothing for a few minutes to let the news sink in.

"I'm sorry to have to ask you, Doctor, but can you tell me anything about Felix's sexual orientation?"

"What? Oh, right. Well. No, not really. At fifteen he was very confused. He talked of a sex change, and I'm pretty sure he was experimenting with homosexuality – but then at that age, we assumed he was just mixed up. Why do you ask?"

"Well, there is some evidence to suggest that he may have had relationships with men."

"It doesn't surprise me, Detective. I'm afraid he chose a very difficult path in life. Maybe now at least he will be at peace."

"I'm very sorry, Dr Lahart. Is there anyone else you think we should notify – his mother perhaps?"

"God, no. She's in New Zealand and hasn't had any contact with any of us for the last five years – not since the settlement. No, it's fine. I'll arrange to come in and identify the remains. If you give me your contact details, I'll get my secretary to be in touch."

Lawler sensed the cool detachment of the man, but presumed that he was quite used to handling death in his professional life. Still, this was his son he was dealing with, and Lawler would have expected a bit more emotion.

Lawler rose from his seat and handed the doctor his card. They then exchanged pleasantries, and Lawler left the house, being glad to get back into his car and out of there.

* * *

Burke had spent a difficult morning with Heffernan. The superintendent was due to go up to the Garda Headquarters in the Phoenix Park in the afternoon, where, he assured the inspector, the matter of budgets, overtime, deployment of manpower and other fiscal issues would be the centre of attention, perhaps with a sprinkling of chat about crime just to keep him happy.

"And remind me, Superintendent, what has all that got to do with catching murderers and drug dealers?" Burke said, exasperated by the direction in which the discussion was going.

"Don't get smart with me, Inspector," the superintendent responded, "if you used the resources we have available more effectively, I probably wouldn't have to go to this bloody thing at all. Do you think I enjoy getting berated by the pen-pushers up there?"

"Sorry, sir. It's just we never seem to have enough of anything to do our jobs properly these days. My team is two men short as it is, and we have a nasty case of double murder on our hands. It's not easy for any of us."

"I know what you mean," the senior man said, softening his approach, "I could probably get you a couple of rookies from Templemore if you're badly stuck."

"More trouble than they are worth, truth be told. No. We'll soldier on with what we've got, but there will be overtime. I can't help that."

"Ah, 'tis all a charade anyway. The bosses know that they'll get more cash from the government if they run out. But they have to go through the motions. There'll be some prick from the department there in a wrinkled grey suit and brown shoes to try and keep us honest, blathering about estimates and overruns, but it's all just for show. Pisses me off."

"So I see, boss."

Heffernan smiled.

"Away with ye then and catch these bloody bandits of yours. Otherwise we'll be getting a grilling about clear-up rates. Who'd be a superintendent, I ask you."

Chapter Twelve

Burke had calmed down a good deal for the afternoon briefing at just after two o'clock. When he had finished with the superintendent, he had nipped across to the pub opposite the station, downed a pint of Guinness and eaten a doorstep of a ham sandwich, and felt the better for it.

"Well, Sergeant, did you get yer man's cigars from the missus?" Burke started off, addressing Moore.

"I got them, boss. But they were at his office. His wife says she couldn't stand the smell in the house. I left them over to forensics. Interesting. The lab technician said that Havana cigars are unusual in that the bit you put in your mouth is sealed. You have to pierce the leaf so the smoke can be drawn in. And McCranny's were already pierced, which she wouldn't expect," Moore said.

"How many did he have?" Dónal Lawler asked.

"There were just four left in the box. He gets them in that fancy shop at the bottom of Grafton Street apparently. Oh, and there's something else. When I was at the office, the architect guy, Freddy Taylor, was in McCranny's office. Apparently, Mrs Mc has asked him to babysit the place for a few weeks."

"Right, thanks Fiona," Burke said, turning to Dónal Lawler.

Moore spoke up again quickly before their attention could be directed to the young detective.

"And there's something else, boss," Moore said. She went on to describe the short tour of the McCranny sites that she had undertaken the previous night, and what she had found at the old warehouse by the river.

"Could be something and nothing. Maybe just some dossers using it to keep in out of the cold. Are you sure it's owned by McCranny?" Burke said.

"Oh, yes. Taylor confirmed it when I spoke to him. But I don't know, sir. The men looked more organised than that, and they weren't badly dressed. Sure, they were in workman's clothes, but not the usual ragtag outfits you'd get with dossers. And they obviously knew each other. They were chatting away merrily in some foreign language or other."

"OK. Well, it might be worth another look if we get time, but for now let's concentrate on the two dead men. Dónal, did you find the young lad's parents?"

"Yes, boss – well, parent actually. I spoke to his father, a Dr Lahart. The boy's mother is in New Zealand apparently. He didn't seem either surprised or too bothered to be honest. Said he was kinda expecting something like this. He obviously wasn't close to his son. He said he hadn't seen him in ages."

"Did you arrange a formal ID of the body?" Burke said.

"Yes. He said his secretary would be in touch to arrange a time."

"Terrific. Right. Plans for the rest of the day. Fiona, you were doing well with those accounts and stuff on McCranny's business. Keep at it, will you? Dig a bit deeper – let's see if there were any other businesses that we don't know of yet. And see if you can explore the payments in and out of the property maintenance company. I'd like to bring blondie in tomorrow for a good grilling. She's been lying to us, so we'll question her under caution. Make sure we have her home address – she won't be at work on Saturday. Dónal, will you follow up with forensics? And see if anyone has recovered anything at all of value from the murder scene. OK. That's it. We're all in tomorrow, by the way. We have to get this sorted out."

When the briefing was over, Moore went to her desk and re-opened the stack of papers that contained the accounts of McCranny's companies. But after a few minutes, she couldn't concentrate. The numbers just seemed to swim around on the pages, and she was unable to focus. Recognising that she needed a change of activity, she logged onto her computer and brought up LinkedIn.

There weren't too many people with the name McCranny on the site, and she soon found the entry for Gerald McCranny of McCranny Construction. Helpfully, LinkedIn provided a short bio for the man, and Moore scrolled down. Many of the entries were connected with the companies that they already knew about, but down near the bottom of the list there was an entry going back a few years that linked McCranny to a haulage company. The firm was called Sprinter Transport Ireland Limited, and there was a photo of a younger Gerald McCranny standing in front of a huge Volvo truck with a silhouette of a thin, agile sprinter running at full pace, painted in black on a panel above the front windscreen.

Moore read the couple of sentences that accompanied the image, but was none the wiser as a result. She then logged out and went to the Company Registration Office website and input the name of the haulage firm. After a moment, the screen filled with information about the company, which was listed as having been established in 2012 with two directors and its registered office care of a solicitor in Tralee, County Kerry. Interestingly, the status of the company was 'Current', meaning that it had not been de-listed and was probably still trading. The most recent entry for accounts and other statutory filings was just over a year ago, and the site encouraged the reader to pay €15 to get a copy of them all, including a list of directors and shareholders. She completed the transaction and a minute later her email pinged to tell her that the reports had been delivered.

Moore printed off the twelve pages of documents pertaining to Sprinter and sat back down at her desk. The other director of the transport company was none other than Freddy Taylor the architect, and the business had turned over just short of €400,000 in the last year. It had fixed assets valued at €120,000 made up mostly of 'vehicles and other equipment', and its balance sheet was healthy, with a surplus of assets over liabilities of €87,000, mostly comprising retained profits transferred from the profit and loss account. Strangely, there were no salaries listed, nor any directors' remuneration, nor were there any of the kind of overheads you would associate with a functioning haulage firm. No rent, wages, telephone or cleaning costs; no postage, stationery, leases or any of the normal stuff that businesses have to pay out. The only costs on the P&L were down to insurance charges, fuel, and depreciation on the vehicles. The accounts were audited by a firm also in Tralee. The two directors were listed as Gerald McCranny and Frederick Taylor, with Taylor doubling up as company secretary. When Moore had finished browsing these documents, she went in search of Burke to report on what she had found.

"So, what?" Burke said dismissively. "He had, or maybe still has, a transport company. Do you think it's significant?"

"Not of itself, but the accounts are bonkers. No wages or salaries, no offices, but it's still making money, so who's driving the trucks?"

"Ah, you know what these companies are like. I'm not surprised their records are incomplete. I can't see an immediate connection to the matter in hand, Fiona. Can you?"

"Well, not immediately, but do you not think it's worth looking into a bit further?"

"I doubt it. I'd prefer if we spent our time looking for evidence. We have two dead bodies and no idea who did it or why. Have we got anything from forensics yet?"

"I'm not sure. Dónal was following that up."

"Well, I want you to follow it up too. We need to get some movement here, Fiona, and soon."

"OK, boss, I hear you."

She went back to her desk, again feeling that Burke had knocked her back. He wasn't letting her use her initiative at all, and she knew she wasn't a bad detective. Then, she had an idea.

Chapter Thirteen

As the working day came to an end, Moore called Dónal Lawler over.

"Fancy a bit of overtime, Dónal?"

"Maybe. What's the gig?"

"I'd like to go back to that old abandoned warehouse and just hang about for a while – see what's going on. I have a feeling there's something not right about it, and it could be connected to McCranny," Moore said.

"Yeah, OK. Sounds like a bit of a long shot, but why not."

Twenty minutes later, Moore and Lawler were seated in Moore's car on the road outside the old rusty gates that led into the warehouse yard. They had parked in between other cars, and in the darkness they were not in the least conspicuous.

"What do you hope to discover, boss?" Lawler asked.

"I don't know, Dónal. That's why we're here, but I have a feeling there's more to this place than meets the eye. Let's just observe for a while and see what gives."

They didn't have very long to wait. At just before seven o'clock, a 7.5 tonne rigid truck came down the road behind where they were parked with its headlights off. Moore picked it up in the driver's mirror, and spotted the words 'Sprinter Transport' sign-written on the front panel. The truck pulled up at the gates to the yard, and the driver got out.

Moore and Lawler scrunched down in their seats to make themselves less obvious, but the driver didn't seem to be bothered about his surroundings too much. He struggled with the old rusty gates for a minute before prising them open enough to get his vehicle into the yard. He got back into it and drove through the gates, then made a wide circle on the old broken surface before bringing the van back to face the gates. He switched the engine off and got out again.

Although neither of the two detectives could now see the rear of the truck, they did see the back doors opening and being folded back against the sides. The next thing they observed were people walking hurriedly in a semi-crouched gait towards the side of the building and then disappearing inside. Moore tried to count them but wasn't certain of the exact number. It wasn't less than eighteen, that was for sure.

"Crikey! I wonder where they have come from," she said to Dónal Lawler.

"God knows. Maybe from a building site somewhere."

"No, I'm thinking further afield. Make sure you get the registration number from the lorry and check it with the ferry companies in the morning to see if it's been anywhere interesting, will you?"

"Yes, sure, boss. But listen. We don't have to go just yet. Let's wait till the truck goes, and then I might just sneak in and have a wee peep at whatever I can find," Lawler said.

"God, I don't know, Dónal, that could be risky. What if you get caught? They could be armed!"

"I'll be careful, boss. I just want to see if I can get close enough to hear them speak. I might recognise the language."

"Well, OK then. I'd better stay here to call in the cavalry if it all goes tits up. Make sure to put your phone on silent, and dim the screen, in case you have to use it."

Lawler made the necessary adjustments to the device.

The van drove from the compound, this time with its headlights blazing. As the driver got out to close the gates, the lights from his vehicle were focused directly on Moore's car, but the man didn't seem to notice anything suspicious, so he carried on, driving away at some speed, leaving a cloud of black diesel fumes in his wake.

Lawler waited a few minutes to make sure that the delivery man wasn't returning. An eerie silence descended on the place. It was a still night, with a little mist beginning to form as the temperature dropped. Moore made sure the interior lights in her car were switched completely off before Lawler opened the door and slid out onto the damp cobbles, closing it gently behind him.

Moore watched as Dónal Lawler crossed the road and slipped in through the gap in the chain-link gates quietly and scurried off down along the side of the building in the shadow of its high walls.

Lawler made his way as silently as he could to the far corner of the old semi-derelict shed. There, he stopped and listened. He could hear the muffled sound of voices inside, but he wasn't sure from exactly what part of the building they were coming. He flattened himself against the wall and eased his head around the corner, so that he could see the entrance. The old wooden door stood ajar, its rotten and broken planks hanging down off the rusted iron hinges at an angle. Lawler eased himself along to the gap, and peeked inside.

There was almost no light, but he could just make out a wooden staircase about five metres away, and it was clear that the muffled voices he could hear were coming from upstairs. Lawler didn't risk tackling the stairs. It would undoubtedly creak, and if he was discovered he would obviously be outnumbered, so he rightly calculated that it wouldn't go well for him. But as he crept towards the foot of the stairs, hoping to hear the men talking more clearly, two people started to descend. He could just see their boots initially, so he quickly ducked around behind the staircase into a sort of cubby hole, hoping that he wouldn't be discovered.

The two men stopped at the foot of the stairs. It was obvious that they were having some form of animated discussion in a language Lawler didn't know. But he was determined not to be defeated. He quietly eased his phone out of his inside jacket pocket, and pressed the 'record' button on the dimly lit screen. He then turned the phone towards the men, hoping that it would record enough of their conversation for him to have it translated back in the office the following day.

The two strangers stood arguing loudly for another ten minutes, and then it seemed some sort of uneasy peace broke out between them, and they went back upstairs, not speaking. As Lawler had predicted, the stairs did indeed creak loudly as the men ascended.

When he was happy that there was no one else about, Lawler extricated himself from the building and reversed his journey back to where Moore was waiting – just starting to get a little apprehensive about her colleague.

Lawler slid back into the passenger seat of the car.

"Well, what's the story?" Moore asked when he was settled.

"I got inside, but all the action was going on upstairs, and I didn't risk it. But I did manage to record a conversation, at least I think I did."

Lawler took out his phone and replayed the few minutes of voice recording.

"It's all Greek to me, or maybe not. But well done, we will be able to get that translated tomorrow back at the station. Make sure you don't erase it. So, is there any more here for us tonight?" Moore said.

"I don't think so, boss, and it's getting really cold. You must be frozen."

"Yeah, I could do with getting the heater going. Let's go."

Chapter Fourteen

Burke had arranged for Moore to collect him at his home in Crumlin at half past eight on the Saturday morning using a marked Garda car. They were going to pick up Sinéad Walsh from her apartment in Ballsbridge and bring her in for questioning.

On the way out to the suburbs Moore filled Burke in on the observations.

Walsh's apartment was in a block of twelve that had been built in the 1980s on a small road off Serpentine Avenue. It was a terrific location, close to the RDS, the DART train service, and the several good restaurants located in the centre of the village. The block looked all of its nearly thirty years of age, with a brown brick façade – fashionable at the time – and balconies with glass fronts, set back into the main living room on each of the six units either side of the entrance. What these dwellings lacked in style, they made up for in size. Each was almost twelve hundred square feet, which was very spacious by today's standards.

At the entrance, twelve doorbells were arranged in a vertical stack. 'Walsh' was written on one of the white paper labels in faded blue biro, indicating that Sinéad occupied apartment number four on the first floor.

Burke gave a long push on Walsh's bell and waited. As he waited, he turned to face Moore who was standing behind him on the path, his breath forming a mist due to the coldness of the air. After what seemed like just a few seconds, he turned back to the door and held his thumb on the bell push for a long time. Eventually, a tired female voice answered, "Yes, who's there?"

Burke announced himself, and heard the woman saying, "For fuck's sake," as she pressed the buzzer on the inside of her apartment to admit the detectives. The interior of the building was warmer, but not by much, and the two climbed the open tread stairs to the first floor. There were two dark brown doors opening off the landing, one each for apartments three and four. As Burke approached door four, it opened and Sinéad Walsh, looking much less glamorous than she had at the office, in a long grey flannel nightshirt and bare feet, walked back inside the room.

Burke and Moore entered, closing the door behind them. The girl disappeared and re-appeared a moment later with a silk navy dressing gown and slippers.

"What the blazes do you two want at this ungodly hour?" she said.

"We need you to come with us to the station, Miss Walsh. We need to ask you some questions," Burke said.

"Can you not just ask me here, and get it over with?"

"No. If you could just get dressed and come with us. Sergeant, would you go with Miss Walsh please?"

Moore and Walsh went into the girl's bedroom. As Sinéad Walsh changed into outdoor clothes, she asked Moore, "Is he always this charming?"

"You've caught him on a good day! You should see him when he's in a bad mood – on the other hand, maybe not," Moore said.

"What's this all about anyway?"

"We just need to clarify a few issues around the things you told us previously. Some of it doesn't seem to add up. It shouldn't take too long if you're straight with us. Best not keep the DI waiting though."

While Sinéad Walsh was completing her ensemble and brushing her long blonde hair, Moore took the opportunity to have a good look around her bedroom. She noticed that there was some very expensive-looking jewellery on the dressing table, and the wardrobe was crammed with an array of expensive clothes.

* * *

When they got to the station, Walsh was shown into an interview room and offered tea or coffee, and asked to wait. Burke and Moore joined her a few moments later.

"Miss Walsh, have you any idea why you are here?" Burke asked.

"None. I've done nothing wrong. Am I under arrest or something?"

"No. Not at present anyway. We just need to ask you a few questions," Moore said.

"Do I need a solicitor?"

"That's up to you, but it's not usual unless you have been arrested. Do you want one?" Burke said.

"No, it's OK. Let's see how it goes. Now can we get on with it please, I don't want to be here all day."

"Yes. Good idea. Miss Walsh, why didn't you tell us that you were a director of one of Gerald McCranny's companies?" Moore said.

"You didn't ask, and anyway, what's that got to do with anything?"

"Maybe nothing, maybe quite a lot," Moore said, opening a chunky manila folder in front of her on the desk.

"I see you have been drawing a significant salary from the Property Management Company too," Moore went on.

"Yes, well, Mr McCranny said it was better for tax reasons if I took most of my pay from that company. I don't really understand all that tax stuff. But I didn't care, as long as I was getting paid."

Moore turned some of the pages from the file around and presented them to the girl.

"Can you explain this to me, Sinéad," Moore said leaning across the table and pointing to a row of figures on the bank statement.

"We would expect to see a property management company receiving a good number of payments in the range of, say, €1,500 to €2,500 clustered around a specific renewal date, or if not that, then monthly equivalent payments. But this company received very large payments sporadically. Can you explain that?"

"No. I don't pay too much attention to the cash flow, to be honest, as long as there's money in the account."

"But didn't you keep the books for the company?" Moore persisted.

"Well, yes, but Gerry, Mr McCranny, looked after a lot of it. He chased any late payments."

"But as a director, as I am sure you know, you have an obligation to know what's going on in the company," Moore said.

Before the girl could reply, Moore pressed on.

"And this entry here for SW Contracts. Several sizeable amounts have been paid out to this company over the last year, but we can't find any trace of a company in that name registered with the Companies Office."

The detectives waited for the girl to reply, but she said nothing. Her cool demeanour was beginning to wobble, and her face became flushed.

"Well?" Burke prompted.

"I... I can't say. I'd need to look it up on our system. I'm sure it's quite in order."

"Miss Walsh, would you have any objection to us looking at your personal bank account details? We can probably get a warrant, but it would speed things up if you just gave us permission," Moore said.

"Look. What's all this about? My boss has just died, and I'm under a lot of strain to try and keep the businesses going. We've had a lot of calls from creditors who are concerned that they won't get paid, and some of them have been quite unpleasant. I'm just doing my job. Can't you leave me alone?"

Sinéad Walsh now became tearful, and took advantage of the box of tissues that had been left on the desk, sniffling loudly. Burke looked at Moore, and nodded imperceptibly. After a moment, when Walsh appeared to be getting her emotions under control, Moore went on, "Is that a yes or a no then?"

Walsh said nothing, but gathered up her things and stood up.

"I am free to leave, am I not?" she said, now fully recovered.

Burke looked at Moore again, this time shaking his head slightly and frowning.

"Yes, of course. But don't leave town, Miss Walsh, we will need to speak to you again."

When Burke and Moore were back up in Burke's office, he said to his colleague, "Well, what did you make of that then?"

"She's a cool customer, there's no doubt. I didn't fall for the little girl lost routine that's for sure. Do you think McCranny was screwing her?"

"Probably not, given that he was gay, or maybe he swung both ways. But I'd say she was screwing him, and not in a sexual way, wouldn't you?"

"Definitely!"

"Right. First thing Monday, I want to organize a thorough search of McCranny's offices. I'll get the Super to organize a warrant, and can you get a few uniformed Gardaí from downstairs and get there early? Take blondie's computer and bring it here. We can get the Technical Bureau to take it apart," Burke said.

"OK, boss. What are you hoping to find?"

"A hypodermic syringe and a bottle of arsenic would be good, but failing that, more information about what is really going on there. The whole thing stinks – and I don't mean the smell of expensive Havana cigars!"

"What are you going to get up to?" Moore said.

"I'm going to do the real police work. Based on what you told me about the old place down by the river, I'm going to get me a few lads from the Armed Response Unit and a few more from Immigration, and I'm going to pay a visit to your favourite warehouse."

"I see. And when are you planning to go calling?"

"About 4 a.m. Monday morning. That's the best time for these kinds of operations," Burke said.

"Oh, right. Why don't I come with you?"

"No, it's OK thanks. You stick to the offices. I'll be fine."

"I wasn't actually concerned about your welfare, boss!"

Burke ignored the sarcasm.

"Right, well I'll just give the Super a call to keep him up to date and get the paperwork straightened out. He's probably away playing golf somewhere. Why don't you get off, and we'll tic-tac on Monday around lunchtime – that's if I don't get myself shot."

"OK, right then. See ya."

Chapter Fifteen

Sunday was a bright, clear, but cool day. Fiona Moore woke at just after eight, and by nine o'clock she was showered and had eaten her breakfast. Moore had recently enrolled on an evening course in photography. She had already been to the first class, and on the strength of a recommendation from the tutor, had gone to Bermingham's Camera Shop on the quays and bought herself a digital single-lens reflex camera made by Nikon. It was an expensive purchase, but the shop assistant, who seemed to know a great deal about the subject, assured her it was the very latest technology with a 24-megapixel sensor that would last her for years, and of course it was a premium brand. The sales girl was particularly effusive about the Nikkor 50mm prime lens that she had been told to get. Moore left the shop several hundred euro lighter, but feeling good that she was now properly equipped for the course.

She had studied the camera's manual at home, but much of it had gone over her head. The instructor from the class had advised her just to set the camera on Auto for the moment, and told her the most important thing to do was to take photographs. He showed her how to hold the camera properly, and focus the lens by half-pressing the shutter release, promising to demonstrate the more advanced features, of which there were many, during a later class.

Moore decided, as it was such a nice day, to wrap up well, and take her new acquisition out in the country to see what she could capture with it.

She set off, driving up along the canal towards the hills that had a light dusting of snow on their peaks. The low winter sun was creating some nice shadows from the trees and buildings, and when she spotted two swans gliding by gently on the water, she stopped the car and got out. The swans obliged, allowing themselves to be photographed against the fine, tall grass along the bank. Moore took several shots and reviewed them on the camera's LCD screen when she was back in the warmth of the car. Two of the pictures were quite good, she thought, and looked forward to presenting them to her teacher at the next class.

She drove on, and soon found herself at the start of the N7, travelling towards the Naas Road. She turned off at Newland's Cross, and drove on past The Square. She turned left, and then right onto the R114 that led up to Bohernabreena. The sun was higher now, but still the light on the frosty fields and the shadows through the trees created interesting, and very photogenic scenes.

She stopped again at a lay-by and got out. It was noticeably colder at this altitude, but she was still able to remove her gloves and operate the camera, grabbing some nice panoramic shots of the city beneath her.

Then she had an idea.

She found Dinny O'Leary's cottage easily enough. It was a small house, nestled down between a little group of pine trees just off the road at the edge of Kiltipper Wood. She recognised the old van that Dinny owned, and pulled up at the side of the road in front of the house. As she pushed open the little metal gate giving her access to the short path up to the front door, a friendly black and white border collie dog came to greet her wagging its tail vigorously. She knocked on the door, and after a moment or two petting the adoring canine, it was opened with a flourish by Dinny O'Leary himself.

"Ah, hello," he said, searching furiously for the woman's name in his memory. "Sergeant... eh... Sergeant..."

"Moore," Fiona said, keen to put the man out of his misery.

"Ah yes," he said, relieved, "come in, won't you. Don't mind the dog. He's harmless."

The front door of Dinny's house opened directly into a good-sized kitchen-living room that was neat and tidy and seemingly well provisioned. A range, not surprisingly burning wood, stood against one wall giving out plenty of heat, and a modern electric oven with four rings and a grill stood beside it. In the middle of the floor was a strong wooden table around which rail-backed kitchen chairs were arranged. The room had two good-sized windows – one to the front adjacent to the door, and one to the rear of the house with a superb aspect out over the woods and to the hills beyond.

"Can I get you a cup of tea?" Dinny asked.

"Yes, thanks, that would be lovely."

Dinny busied himself filling the kettle from one of the brass taps over the Belfast sink under the back window. He lifted the lid on the right-hand side of the range, and placed the kettle down on the hot iron plate.

"This won't take long now. The range is good and hot. Sit ye down there, Sergeant. What has you up in these parts on a Sunday, anyway?"

"Ah, I was out for a drive with my camera, and I thought I'd just call in to see how you were. That business of the lad in the hut must have given you a bad fright."

"It did, to be sure. I've never seen anything the like of it. Have you found out who did for the poor fella yet?"

"Well, our enquiries are ongoing. Is there any word around here about it?"

"Nothing much. Just the usual gossip," Dinny said as he busied himself preparing their drink.

"I'm afraid I don't have any biscuits. I have to go down to the shops later when I get myself sorted out," Dinny said.

"Just as well. I can't afford to put on any weight."

"Go away out of that! Sure, haven't you a grand figure the way you are."

Moore was amused by the man's rather clumsy attempt to flirt with her, but she took the compliment anyway.

"So, tell me, Dinny, do you work on your own up here all the time?"

"Ah, no. In the winter it's just me and another fella – Paddy Dunne. Himself and myself manage the place when there's nothing else going on. But in the summer, it's all go. Teams of lads come in with their machinery to thin the trees and take them away to the sawmills in Dublin or Glenealy, and the place gets fair busy. But I prefer it when it's quiet, like now."

"I suppose you have to get on well with Paddy. Where does he live anyway?"

"He has a cottage about another mile along up towards the hills, going towards Ticknock. It's not much of a place, to be honest, but he seems to like it. He tells me he enjoys the solitude."

"And are you both single?"

"We are, to be sure. When I sees the trouble that some of the men get into with wives and families, all costing a fortune to keep going, I don't envy them. I'm better off on my own."

"But it must get lonely all the same?" Moore said.

"Not really. I like my own company, and I'm used to it now anyway. I've got the dog for company, and he never asks me for anything except a bowl of food and a walk across the fields."

Moore could see that the man had a point, and he seemed to her to be quite content.

"Do you go down the town for a drink now and then?"

"I do. But you have to be careful with all this drink driving nonsense they've brought in lately. But you'd know all about that," he said, giving her a sideways glance.

"I leave all that to the uniformed crew. I've more to be doing than harassing a few solitary bachelors that might be a bit over the limit."

Dinny relaxed when he heard this. Obviously, he was used to navigating his old van along the country lanes after he had had a few pints.

They carried on chatting about this and that for another twenty minutes or so while they drank their tea. Moore got the impression that despite the man's self-imposed solitude, he was glad of the company. When it seemed like the right time, Moore excused herself and said goodbye to him.

When she was back in her car, she drove away from Dinny's house and pulled into a gateway. She made a phone call to Tallaght Garda station, and asked the duty sergeant to look up a Paddy Dunne living near Bohernabreena, and give her the exact address.

A moment later, she was tapping the Eircode into her sat-nav which indicated that Dunne's house was indeed a little over a mile further on, just as Dinny had said.

* * *

Paddy Dunne's house was the exact opposite of Dinny O'Leary's. It was dilapidated, with all kinds of junk dotted here and there around the unkempt front garden. The house was in poor repair too, with broken gutters; dirty, streaky walls that had once been white; and peeling paint on all of the visible woodwork. The windows were filthy, and the old iron gate leading to the house from the road was rusting and hanging off its hinges.

Moore waited in her car for a few minutes just to observe. There was no smoke coming from the single chimney, so she decided to get out and have a look around.

She approached the front door, being careful to avoid the bits of old iron lying about in the so-called garden, and rapped on the rotting wood. There was no response, and no sound from within, so she rapped again, and called out Dunne's name.

Still, there was no response, so she gently pushed on the door and to her surprise found that it wasn't locked or in any way secured.

"I don't suppose he needs to worry about burglars anyway," she said to herself, "who'd be bothered?"

The door creaked open. Things inside the house were just as disorderly and decrepit as outside. Moore called out Dunne's name again, but getting no reply, she decided to go in.

"Probable cause, here goes!" she said to herself.

Inside the house, the smell of old, stale food and dirt was pungent. The kitchen was a mess, and Moore could hardly believe that anyone could live in such squalor, and she had seen some grotty living accommodation in her time. Every surface was covered in detritus of one kind or another, and the single tap in the sink was dripping constantly down onto a pile of dirty dishes.

Moore donned vinyl gloves, more to protect herself from infection than anything else, and started to look through the stuff on the table and dresser. She had an instinctive feeling there was something here worth finding. On the old dresser, under a brown paper bag with the remains of takeaway food growing a particularly colourful fuzz of mould, there was a striped tea towel, folded into a neat square, which Moore felt was incongruous, given the disarray of the rest of the crap. She moved the paper bag and unfolded the tea towel. Inside, there was a large red-handled kitchen knife with a wide blade, and it was smeared with what looked to Moore like blood.

Moore realised that the find could well be significant, although there could also be a perfectly innocent explanation. Dunne might, after all, hunt in the surrounding woods, and catch rabbits which he might butcher at home and cook. Or there could be a much more sinister story behind it. She realised that she couldn't just take the knife away with her. It would be inadmissible as evidence, given how it had been obtained, but there was something she could do. She nipped back out to her car and retrieved her Nikon camera. Back in Dunne's house, she took several photographs of the knife from a number of different angles, and then a host of other shots of the room. At least if Dunne did away with the weapon before she could get back officially, she would have some evidence of its existence. When she had finished playing photographer, she wrapped the knife back up in the towel and replaced the rancid brown bag where she had found it.

She left the house undisturbed, and once outside and a safe distance away she called Aidan Burke to tell him what she had found. They agreed that the following morning she should get a warrant from Superintendent Heffernan and come back to search Dunne's house officially to remove the knife. The search of McCranny's offices could wait for a day or two, or if she felt like it, Moore could delegate that task to Dónal Lawler.

Chapter Sixteen

Burke had agreed to rendezvous with the Armed Response Unit at Store Street station at half past three in the morning on Monday. It was bitterly cold, with crystals of white frost glistening on the footpaths. He had secured two units from the ARU which gave him eight armed officers in all. The team was led by Inspector Mick Tyrrell, and in accordance with Garda protocol, he would have operational control during the raid. Burke, therefore, was merely an observer.

Tyrrell and Burke held a brief meeting to make sure that they were both on the same page, as it were. They also had two Transit vans full of uniformed Gardaí from the Immigration Unit. By ten to four they were prepared, and set off across the river and down along the southern quays towards the old warehouse. The blue flashing lights and exhaust fumes from their vehicles made an eerie sight in the still, early morning air.

The lead jeep drove straight over the old chain-link gates, followed by the second ARU vehicle. The Transits remained outside, as did Burke, awaiting the all clear from the armed officers. The ARU men sprinted along the side wall of the building, barely visible in the dark, dressed in their all-black jumpsuits and baseball caps. They held their Heckler & Koch MP7 sub-machine guns braced against their shoulders as they ran. Two officers went into the building and up the stairs, while the others remained at the ready on the ground floor. Two more had gone around to the back of the building in case anyone tried to escape by jumping out into the river.

"Armed Police – stay where you are, Armed Police," they shouted as they invaded the rudimentary dormitory that was occupied by twenty or more sleepy foreigners. Most of the men slept on thin mattresses scattered around the floor with sleeping bags over them. One or two men had the relative luxury of low-slung camp beds. The officers stood guard over the beds, having instructed the men to stay down, while another three came up the stairs and searched for weapons. They found plenty of builders' tools – wrecking bars, lump hammers, stone chisels and so on – but no actual weapons. After a few minutes they gave the all clear to the men outside, and the rest of the Garda swarmed into the building.

Still under the watchful eye of the ARU, the immigration officers started to interrogate the men one by one, but it was very difficult, as most of them appeared to have very little English. It soon became clear that none of them had any proper papers. After twenty minutes, one of the men was singled out as being a little more fluent than any of the others, so the Gardaí focused their attention on him. His name was Bilal Demir, and he was, as they had suspected, Turkish.

The Gardaí called for transport for their captives, and fifteen minutes later three more Transit mini-buses rolled into the yard. Burke was now face to face with Demir, and was beginning to interrogate him.

"How did all these men get here, Bilal?"

"I came from Turkey by boat to Greece and onwards overland to France. Then I was met by a lorry in France and brought here," Demir said.

"Who made the arrangements for you?"

"Many men. All of us paid a lot of money to secure our journey, and we will be paying back for a long time," Bilal said in broken English.

"OK. Well, we're going to take you back to the local police station now, and we will continue to question you there. We can arrange legal representation for you and the others there, if you think you need it."

"What? You are not going to beat us?" Bilal asked.

"Well, we can arrange it if you think it's absolutely necessary, but we don't usually beat up the people we are questioning. But we need you to provide us with information about this arrangement," Burke said.

When all of the immigrants had been taken away to three different Garda stations in the centre of the city, the ARU was stood down. Burke thanked Inspector Tyrrell for his help, and then spent the next hour rummaging through the men's meagre possessions. They had very few personal items – just a few spare clothes, some letters written in a language Burke didn't recognise, and a small amount of cash in euro notes stashed among their bed clothes.

He left the site in the care of two uniformed Gardaí with instructions that if anyone else turned up, they were to be detained, though he doubted that would happen.

* * *

When Burke returned to the office later in the morning he put a call through to the Immigration Unit and asked for Inspector Ann Quinlan. He had worked with her before, and found her to be pragmatic and thorough. He explained the situation to her, and asked that she come across to Store Street while he conducted a formal interview with Bilal Demir. Inspector Quinlan said that she would be glad to help, and asked if he thought an interpreter was needed.

"I don't think so, Ann. He seems to have reasonable English – or at least he did when we lifted him. Of course, he could clam up on us, but let's see how it goes. We can always get someone in if it proves necessary. How soon can you get here?"

"I'll be about twenty minutes. See you then."

Ann Quinlan arrived equipped with two cups of takeaway coffee. They sat in Burke's office to prepare for the interview.

"So, what's the story with this Demir character then, Aidan?"

Burke told the immigration officer all about the raid on the old warehouse.

"Hmm, interesting. At the very least we need to find out exactly where they are from, and what they are doing here. Do you think they're working?" Quinlan asked.

"Yes, I do. My sergeant carried out an observation on the warehouse the other night, and they all came trooping back in after hours. There was quite a collection of tools in the place too. They're working all right. What I want to know is who for, and if whoever it is had anything to do with getting them here."

"Let's go and find out then."

* * *

The Turkish man was, as Burke had predicted, much less free with his conversation when they sat down opposite him in the interview room. He confirmed his name, but then he pretended that he couldn't understand what Quinlan was saying, and just shrugged his shoulders in response to each of the woman's questions.

"Look, Bilal, this won't do at all. We know you have perfectly good English. Now you'd better start answering our questions, or things will get pretty rough for you. At the very least, you will be deported."

The Turk looked Burke in the eye for a long moment before speaking.

"So? I just come back again," he said.

Burke looked at Quinlan and shook his head imperceptibly.

"Not if we deport you to Damascus, Bilal. You won't get out of there so handily, will you?"

The man visibly flinched in response to this idea.

"You can't do that. It's illegal!"

"So are you – illegal, Bilal. I can do what I like. There is no one to protect you here."

Burke let the prospect sink in before leaning forward and softening his voice.

"Of course, there is another way, Bilal."

"What do you mean?"

"Do you have family out there in Turkey?"

"Yes, of course. I have a wife and two small children. That's why I am here – to work, and send money back to them so they can have a better life. You have no idea how difficult things are there for them. They have nothing. Nothing at all."

"Yes, I can imagine. It must be dreadful. Of course, it would be very different for them if they could all come here and be with you. You could settle down as a family. Get your children a good education, a house, a proper job with good pay. Perhaps your wife could get a job too. Sound good?"

"You are joking with me, Inspector. How is this possible?"

Burke glanced at Ann Quinlan again, who was looking decidedly uneasy.

"Bilal. If you co-operate with us, and tell us all you know about what's really going on, then I'll see what can be done for you and your family. I have plenty of influence in certain quarters, and, well, just one more family on top of the many hundreds of migrants we have taken in already shouldn't be too difficult to arrange. What do you say?"

"And what about the others?" Bilal said.

Quinlan decided she had better intervene before Burke promised to give them all some kind of amnesty – a promise she knew he could not deliver.

"There's nothing we can do for them, I'm afraid. They will have to go back," she said.

"But if we knew where they had come from, and under what circumstances, we might be able to return them to the country where they first arrived – say, France, for instance. Isn't that right, Inspector Quinlan?" Burke added hastily.

"How do I know you are not trying to trick me?" Bilal asked. "I don't trust police, and I have good reason."

"You don't, Bilal. But it's not how we operate. We are not like the police in your country. We do what we say."

Bilal leaned forward and buried his head in his hands. Burke knew to stay quiet as the man processed his options. Could he turn down the opportunity that the policeman was offering? But on the other hand, if word got back to his homeland that he had been helping the authorities in Ireland, his family could be in real danger.

He looked up.

"OK, OK. I will answer your questions, but you must promise what you say is true – that you will arrange for my family to come here and join me, and all the rest."

"Just tell us what you know, Bilal."

Chapter Seventeen

When Fiona Moore arrived at work on Monday morning, she went directly to Superintendent Heffernan's office. He wasn't in, but his clerical assistant had the warrant that she needed to return to Paddy Dunne's house and collect the knife that she had found there the previous day.

When she got downstairs, she briefed Dónal Lawler.

"Dónal, I need you to go and carry out the search on McCranny's office. Take four or five uniformed officers with you and make a damn nuisance of yourself. Do a very thorough search, and don't take any shit from them. I want the computers brought back here, and we're also looking for a hypodermic syringe, with or without a phial of arsenic, so you see how thorough you need to be."

"Jesus, boss, you're not joking, are you?"

Moore just smiled at the young detective, and said, "I'm off. I'll see you later."

"Where are you going, boss?" Lawler called after her, but she was already on her way.

Moore drove out on the now well-worn route along the canal, up the Long Mile Road and onto the Naas Road at the Red Cow, turning left at Newland's Cross. She passed

Tallaght on her right-hand side, and continued as the land rose up, leaving the densely populated areas behind her.

It was a clear, bright morning, and the low winter sun created dappled shadows through the trees as the forest began to take over the landscape. She passed Dinny O'Leary's house, noting that his old green van was nowhere to be seen. She took this as a good sign. Hopefully, the two men would be busy in the woods, and she wouldn't encounter any trouble. She would have liked to have had at least one other officer with her, but with everything that was going on, resources were scarce.

Moore pulled the car up beyond the nearly derelict cottage, and waited. Again, there was no smoke coming from the chimney. Neither was there any sign of a vehicle that might belong to Dunne.

"So far, so good," she said to herself.

She got out of the car, and pulled her jacket tightly around her. It was a lot colder at this altitude than it had been in the centre of town. She made her way to the front door of the house, warrant in hand, keeping her eyes peeled and her senses tuned for the presence of anyone else.

When she reached the old front door, she was dismayed to find it locked. She could have shouldered it open quite easily – the rotting wood would have yielded readily to the slightest pressure, but she didn't want to break in. She walked around the side of the house, trampling down the tall nettles that threatened to sting her ankles, and being careful to climb over the various bits of rusted iron that festooned the so-called garden. At the back of the house, there was another wooden door that was in much the same condition as the one at the front. The bottom of the door was wavy, where some of the wood had given in to rot, and the paint that had once been dark green was now largely peeled away. Moore pushed the door gently inwards, and much to her relief it scraped open along the granite step.

Inside, the house was as musty and fetid as she had remembered from her earlier visit. She side-stepped over to the draining board where the brown paper bag containing the remnants of a Chinese meal was still sitting on top of the filthy tea towel. She carefully unwrapped the towel, and was relieved to see that the knife was still there just as she had left it. She used her vinyl gloves to lift the knife clear and place it in a large evidence bag. She then retraced her steps, but before leaving the property altogether, she wedged the warrant into a gap between the boards of the old front door.

"There you go – all nice and legal now," she said, and hurried back to the safety of her car.

Moore placed the knife in its bag on the floor in the passenger's footwell and drove to the Garda forensic laboratory, attached to Garda Headquarters in the Phoenix Park. When she got there, she sought out Eleanor McHugh, whom she had worked with previously.

"Hi, Ellie, how's things?"

"Oh, hello Fiona. What have you got there for me?"

"It's a knife that may have been involved in a murder that we are investigating. Could you have a look at it for prints? And I think there may be some blood on it. We need to see if it's a match to one Felix Lahart that Dr O'Higgins has in the mortuary."

"OK, give it here. I presume it's urgent, as usual."

"Of course, isn't it always?" Moore said smiling.

"OK. I'll fast-track it for you. I might have something by close of business," Ellie said.

"It's well for some – close of business indeed!"

"Well, you know what I mean."

"Thanks. Catch you later," Moore said.

* * *

When Moore got back to Store Street, she was told that Burke was busy with Bilal Demir, so she went in search of Dónal Lawler.

"Hi, Dónal. How did the search of McCranny's offices go?" she said when she found him surrounded by several desktop PCs and a number of files all stacked up beside his desk.

"It's still going on. They were furious. That guy Taylor was hopping mad. All the usual guff about police harassment, and 'Your superiors will be hearing about this' etc etc. But I think he's all mouth and trousers, boss."

"Only to be expected, I suppose. What about the lovely Sinéad?"

"She's a cool customer, that one. She said almost nothing. But I did notice her on her mobile phone once or twice. We couldn't take that from her – she said it was her private property, and hence not covered by the warrant."

"Bugger that! I'd have had it off her. Still, all in good time. We can get her records from the phone company if we need them. No need to ask what you'll be doing for the next few hours. Have you got someone from the Park to help you with the tech stuff?"

"Yes, Jane is coming down. We'll go through the computers together and see what we can find." The woman he was referring to was Jane Langford, a brilliant technical expert from the ever-growing Garda Technical Bureau based in the Phoenix Park. Jane had worked with Burke's team on a previous case, and was held in high esteem for her ability to find data no matter how well hidden the owner thought that it was.

"Great. Concentrate on the property maintenance company to start with, and then see if you can find anything on Sprinter Transport. There's something iffy about that outfit for sure. We'll have a briefing later when Aidan is finished with his Turkish friend."

"Right, boss. I'll get on then."

As Moore was walking away, she remembered about the cigars and the poison.

"Oh, Dónal, I don't suppose you found a syringe anywhere, did you?"

"No, boss. No sign of anything like that."

"Hmph. OK, thanks."

When she got back to her desk, Moore could hear an animated conversation coming from Burke's office. She didn't exactly eavesdrop, but she couldn't help hearing the drift of the conversation all the same.

"You shouldn't have promised to bring his family over for him. You know that's not going to happen, Inspector," Ann Quinlan said.

"Look, Inspector, I have two murders to solve, and as a result of our investigations, you have a couple of busloads of illegals to your name. Frankly, I don't give a shit about Demir or his family. I need results, and I'll get them any way I can. Understood?"

"Oh, I understand all right. But you have no idea how politically sensitive these things can be. We deal with them all the time, and I can tell you, once the politicians get involved, your investigation will be the last thing on their mind. You'll be lucky if you're not directing traffic in Cahirciveen for the rest of your career when that little stunt of yours gets out."

Burke looked the woman in the eye.

"There isn't any traffic in Cahirciveen. You needn't worry about me. I'm half thinking of chucking it in anyway."

Quinlan wasn't expecting that.

"I see. Well, you'll be around for a week or two yet, I suppose, so we'd better see what we can salvage from this for now. What's your plan?"

"I want to let Demir contemplate his options for a few hours. Then I'm going back in – see what he can come up with. Are you going to hang around?"

"I sure am. And promise me one thing, Aidan – no more tricks. I'm just as keen as you are to get information on where these lads have come from, and in particular, who is behind it all. If we can get that information, we may be able to round up a few of the big fish. Now that would be a feather in both our caps!"

"Look, Ann, I'll do what I have to do. You play it your way and let me get on with it my own way. And if things go tits up, you can come and visit me in County Kerry – I hear it's quite nice during the summer months!"

"Jesus, Aidan, you're impossible," Quinlan said, but she was smiling, despite herself.

Chapter Eighteen

"Moore," the detective said, answering the phone.

"Hi, Fiona. It's Ellie here. You know that knife you gave me?"

"Hi, Ellie, yes of course. What gives?"

"Well, we got lots of prints from the handle, but no matches in our database, I'm afraid. But here's the interesting thing. It was blood on the blade, OK."

"And?" Moore said.

"Vulpes. Or to be more accurate, Vulpes vulpes. The red fox. They are very common here. They even come into town at night and scavenge around in the bins left out by the pubs and restaurants. Where did you get the knife?"

"A fox! Wow, I never thought of that. I retrieved it from an old woodman's cottage up in the Dublin Mountains."

"That figures. They cause a lot of damage to small trees. He probably kills quite a few of them. I'm not certain, but I think there may still be a reward for a dead one. It used to be ten shillings if you brought in the fox's tail to a police station."

"Charming! Oh well, thanks anyway. There goes my favourite theory. Thanks for getting back to me so quickly," Moore said.

"No worries. See ya."

* * *

Burke brought the briefing together at five o'clock as promised. Ann Quinlan was in attendance as well as Moore and Lawler. Jane Langford was still probing the computers that had come in from McCranny's office, but she wasn't far away if she was needed.

Burke started by explaining the position regarding the raid on the old warehouse, and how they appeared to have the ringleader, or gang master, in custody downstairs.

"What's the plan, boss? Has he given us anything useful yet?" Moore asked.

Burke looked at Quinlan before replying to his sergeant.

"I'm working on him, Fiona. It's not easy to frighten these types. They've seen more horror in the border areas of Syria and Turkey than we can ever imagine. I'm working on some different tactics at the moment. We'll see how successful they are later. I'll be continuing to question him when this meeting is over. Anything from any of the other lads we brought in?"

"Nothing of value. Firstly, they don't seem to have any English, and anyway they are just the foot soldiers. We're questioning them of course, but I don't expect much of a breakthrough," Ann Quinlan said.

"You should ask the inspector to lend a hand," Moore said mischievously.

"What about the knife you found up the mountains?" Burke said, anxious to move the discussion on quickly.

"Fox blood, I'm afraid, and lots of John Doe prints. Useless," Moore said.

"Terrific! I hope you have better news, Dónal?"

"Not really, boss. Jane is still working on the computers we brought back from McCranny's offices. Taylor is hopping mad. He's gone off to find a politician to bend his ear about police harassment."

"That shouldn't take him long. Great. I'll await the call from Heffernan! Look, folks. We're spinning our wheels. We have two dead bodies, for God's sake. And at least as far as the young lad is concerned, I don't think we're dealing with master criminals here. We need to make some progress and quickly. I want you all to go back over everything we have to date. We've obviously missed something important, or maybe several things," Buke said, trying to contain his frustration.

"Like what, boss?" Moore asked.

"Like what's the connection between McCranny and Lahart, for example, Sergeant? Could McCranny have bumped off the rent boy to conceal his peccadillo? Was Lahart threatening to blackmail him, or maybe actually doing it? Where's the real weapon that was used on the boy? C'mon everybody – we're supposed to be detectives – do some fucking detecting!"

The meeting broke up. Lawler went back to where Jane Langford was working on the PCs.

"Cripes, Dónal, is he always like that?" she said.

"No, not always. He gets very frustrated when things aren't moving though. It's usually Fiona that gets it in the neck. Anyway, have you got anything?"

"Well, not a lot, but I'd say the property management company is definitely fronting something. The accounts don't make any sense at all. Loads of money sloshing about, but none of it looks legit. It'll take me a good few hours to put a pattern together. I'd better stay on for a while. I don't want Burke screaming at me too for not being conscientious!"

"Ah, don't mind him. His bark is worse than his bite. But I know what you mean. Anything on the Sprinter company?"

"I haven't got to that yet. Here – you could have a go if you like. There're a few folders on that one over there," Langford said, pointing to one of the other black computer towers that they had collected from McCranny's offices, "the files were encrypted, but I found the key easily enough, and I've left them open."

"OK. Thanks. I'd enjoy that," Lawler said.

* * *

Burke went back downstairs to continue his questioning of Bilal Demir. He tried to shake Ann Quinlan off by telling her that the traffic would be getting bad, and if she wanted to get home at a sensible hour, she should probably leave at once.

"It's fine, I'm in no hurry. Anyway, someone needs to keep an eye on you, Inspector," she said, smirking slightly.

"Do ya think?" he replied.

When they were seated in the interview room, Burke addressed Demir.

"Well, Bilal, you have had some time to think about the situation. Are you going to tell us what this is all about now?"

"The things you said about my family – are they true? Can you really bring my wife and children to Ireland to be here with me? Will I be able to work and earn money to feed them, house them, educate my kids?"

Quinlan tapped Burke's foot gently under the table.

"That all depends on you, Bilal. If you can help us to get to the bottom of this – round up the people behind it, then anything is possible. Isn't that right, Inspector Quinlan?"

Ann Quinlan shifted uneasily in her seat. She didn't want to become part of Burke's extravagant promises, but she was just as anxious as he was to find out who was behind what looked very much like trafficking, and bring them to justice.

"We will be very grateful for anything you can do to help us, Bilal. Be assured."

Bilal was used to being lied to by the authorities. When he lived in Turkey, he has been arrested several times, and badly beaten when the Turkish police believed that he had information about cross-border people smuggling. The last time he was incarcerated, he actually feared for his life. Things had changed in Turkey. Since Trump had seemingly turned on President Erdogan, the police had become much more aggressive, and the rule of law had teetered on a complete breakdown. People were disappearing without notice or due cause, and it was at this stage that Bilal decided to jump ship, as it were, and take his chances with the traffickers.

"OK, I will help you then. I trust you."

"Thank you, Bilal. You are doing the right thing," Quinlan said.

"So, where do I start?"

For the next two hours, the young Turk poured out his story. He had managed to contact a group in Istanbul who he heard were arranging safe passage to Europe. He met two of them in a café, and they agreed to get him to Germany, where they said the doors were almost wide open for refugees, for a price. Ten thousand Turkish Lira was demanded, which of course Bilal didn't have. But his wife had some gold jewellery that her grandmother had left her, and reluctantly he sold it on the black market and raised the money. He even had a few hundred euro left over to get him started when he reached Germany.

Bilal never knew the names of the two men he had met who had arranged his passage. He was to meet a large forty-foot lorry at the edge of his town at two o'clock in the morning on a particular day, and he would be placed in the back for the journey to Europe. He was told to bring warm clothes, a supply of water and some food, as the trip would take two days, and he might not be alone. The journey would take him to Istanbul, then into Bulgaria, on through Serbia into Hungary. From there, the truck would skirt the Slovakian border before entering Czechia and travelling on into Germany stopping south of Dresden. He would be met in Germany, and travel to France would be arranged at that point.

He kept the rendezvous with the lorry at the appointed location along with four other men that he didn't know. They climbed into the back of the trailer, and hid amongst the pallets of Beko electrical goods, which from the shape of the boxes, he guessed were fridges or freezers. The lorry wasn't cold, but it was stuffy, with just a small ventilation grill at the front where fresh air mixed with quite a strong whiff of diesel fumes came in.

The truck travelled smoothly, and seemed to traverse the various frontier posts with consummate ease. As promised, some forty-four hours later they arrived in Germany where the truck stopped in a large warehouse complex and the back door was opened.

When Bilal and his fellow travellers had disembarked, they were met by a shady-looking character in a black leather jacket and a woolly hat, who said that he was fixing up the next part of the trip, but that it would cost the men €200 each. A row ensued, and one of Bilal's companions produced a knife which he used to stab the guy in the leather jacket.

When this happened, Bilal fled into the dense forest surrounding the warehouses and hid there for three days. He had no food, but he was able to find water in some small pools and a little stream that trickled down amongst the trees. Then he took a chance. He went back onto the road and hitched a ride north-west to Berlin. He still had no papers, but using his wits, he soon found where the Turkish enclaves were located in the Kreuzberg area of the city, and once there amongst his countrymen, he was sheltered from the authorities. After a few more days, his new friends introduced him to an Irishman who arranged a lift for him to France. The man advised Bilal to avoid

Calais, and go instead to Cherbourg. In Cherbourg, he was to stay close to the ferry boarding area and watch out for a truck with 'Sprinter' written on the front of it. He should get into the back of this truck and hide himself amongst the cargo. He was told there could be other men inside the van too, but they were not a threat.

Bilal waited for forty-eight hours in Cherbourg, concealing himself between the buildings. He managed to scavenge some food from the bins left out by the restaurant at the ferry port, and at night, when the last ship had departed, he found a door that let him into the terminal where he could doss down and stay warm.

On the third day, he was just beginning to wonder if the whole thing was a hoax, and he had parted with the last of his money to a scam artist, when he spotted the van with 'Sprinter' written on the front, queueing up to board the ship, just as his associate in Berlin had said. He hung around until the driver went into the terminal to sort out tickets or get some food, and then he cautiously opened the rear door of the big van and slid inside. There were three other men already in the vehicle, but apart from nodding a greeting to him, they said nothing.

The ferry crossing was lumpy, and one of the other men was quite violently seasick, making the atmosphere in the enclosed space smelly and uncomfortable, but Bilal had no choice. He had to remain there. The ship eventually arrived in Rosslare, and the Sprinter van drove off. When it had travelled several miles, the van pulled onto a small, narrow lane, and the man who had been sick got out. The rest of the stowaways remained where they were. The van travelled on further, and by nightfall, although Bilal couldn't tell the time in the enclosed, windowless space, they had reached a city where the truck stopped and started frequently, and traffic noises could be heard outside. The truck then stopped, and the driver opened the rear door. Bilal and his travelling companions jumped down, glad to be out of the stench and rancid atmosphere inside the vehicle.

A man in a suit greeted them. Bilal was told his name was Mr Freddy, and that the next day he would come and bring them to a place where they would work on a building site. They could stay in the building beside where the truck had parked, and they would be paid €200 every Thursday in cash, if they worked hard and told no one where they were from.

"This Mr Freddy, Bilal, what does he look like?" Burke asked.

"Tall, thin and always in a business suit."

"And how long have you been working for him?"

"Many weeks now. And we always get paid every Thursday. I can get to the Western Union office on Saturday and send half back to my family. It's good."

"Except that it's highly illegal, Bilal. OK, for now you must stay here with us. Tomorrow, I want you to go with one of my officers and show him where exactly you have been working. Don't worry about your safety – we will look after you now."

Burke nodded to Ann Quinlan, and they got up and left the interview room. On the walk back to his office, Burke said to Quinlan, "Quite a story, poor bugger."

"Believe me, I've heard much worse. He's lucky he has English, and he's smart too. Lots of them end up in a lot more difficulty. Are you going to be able to keep your promise to him?"

"We'll see. I'm more interested in getting face to face with 'Mr Freddy' for now. Bilal will keep. Can you find out if they have got any additional information from the others that were brought in? I have a few things to arrange."

"Yes, OK. We can talk later."

Chapter Nineteen

"Fiona. Just a sec. Listen. I want you to take Dónal and a few uniformed Gardaí round to McCranny's offices and bring in Freddy Taylor and blondie. It looks as if they're up to their necks in people trafficking, so you needn't be too gentle with them. OK?"

"Yes, boss. What have you found out?" Moore said.

"Later. Just get going for now, will you?"

Moore said nothing, but turned on her heels and went in search of Dónal Lawler. They commandeered a couple of uniformed Gardaí who were down in the canteen having their break, and left Store Street in two separate marked squad cars with blue lights flashing and sirens cutting through the morning traffic. They skidded to a halt outside McCranny's office building, and all four dashed in and up the stairs to the office.

Melissa was seated behind the reception desk as usual, reading a magazine. The telephone was off the hook, the receiver being left down on her desk away from the rest of the equipment. When they came charging in, she looked up, but didn't appear to be particularly alarmed.

"Morning, Melissa. We need to speak to Mr Taylor, and now would be good," Moore said.

"I'm sorry, Sergeant, you're out of luck. Mr Taylor hasn't shown up today. But I can leave a message to say you were looking for him, if you like?" the girl said calmly, ever the efficient receptionist.

"Is Sinéad in her office?" Moore said, nodding to one of the uniformed men to go and have a look around.

"No. Same story, I'm afraid. It's just little old me here today, and to be honest, I don't know why I'm here at all. I might not even get paid!"

"Where are they, Melissa?" Moore asked.

"No idea. They were here on Friday, all business-like. But no sign of them today."

"Have they phoned in?" Lawler said.

"Nope. But I have the phone disconnected anyway. I was getting too many horrid phone calls from the subbies and suppliers. Right rude some of them were. One of them even threatened to come around and sort me out! Honestly – some people."

"Have you a mobile phone number for Taylor?" Moore said.

"Yes, of course."

Melissa wrote the number on a yellow Post-it sticker and handed it over to Moore. She called it, but a message informed her that the phone was no longer in use.

"I need Sinéad's number too," Moore said.

The procedure was repeated with the same result. Moore drew Lawler aside.

"Dónal, go outside and call the boss. Tell him Taylor and the girl have gone AWOL. He'll know what to do."

"Right, boss."

"Melissa, can I have word in private?" Moore said.

"Sure," she said. She got up, and the two women went into what had been McCranny's office and closed the door.

"Listen, Melissa, we have reason to believe that Mr Taylor, and perhaps Sinéad Walsh as well, may have been engaged in some activity involving the employment of illegal immigrants. Do you know anything about that?"

"No! Of course not. I'm just the receptionist."

"You've never heard them talking about anything like that?"

"No, never. Do you think it has anything to do with Mr McCranny's death?" Melissa said.

"We don't know. But we need to talk to both of them urgently. Have you any idea where they might be?"

"No, but I can get their home addresses from the file, if you wait a minute. I know where they are kept."

"Yes, please. As quick as you like."

Melissa went back outside to the front office and retrieved a file from one of the cabinets.

"Here you go," she said and handed them over.

Moore took the file and gave it to Lawler.

"Get onto this pronto. See if either of them is at home, and if so, bring them in, OK?"

"Yeah, sure, boss."

* * *

Aidan Burke was upstairs appraising Superintendent Heffernan of developments.

"Jesus, Aidan, that's a right old hornet's nest you're after stirring up there. Are you getting any closer to sorting out the man's murder?" Heffernan said.

"No, not really, sir. I'm sure the whole thing is connected, but exactly how escapes me for the moment."

"What about the young lad in the woods? Anything there?"

"We thought we had a likely suspect for that one, sir, but it turned out to be a dead end, if you'll excuse the pun." Burke didn't want to tell his boss that they had found what they thought was the murder weapon, only to discover that it had been smeared with animal blood.

"Look, Aidan, I know it's all very exciting to be dealing with people trafficking and overseas connections and all that malarkey, but we have people for that. Leave it to the immigration folks. You just concentrate on the two murders. If there's a connection to the foreigners, it will come out in the wash. I need some results on these deaths. The press boys are starting to turn on us – you know the kind of thing, 'Gardaí can't see the wood for the trees in forestry killings'," Heffernan said, drawing an imaginary headline in the air in front of him with his fingers. "I'm getting fierce stick from the Park. We need some sort of breakthrough, and soon."

"Yes, sir." Burke knew better than to argue with the Cork man when he was in this kind of humour.

"Do you need any more resources? More men?"

"No, thank you, sir. We need more evidence, that's all."

"Well, I can't help you with that. But I need you to keep me up to date every day on this till you get it sorted. I'll try and keep the Commissioner and the television away from it for a few days, but don't let me down, Aidan. Now, away with you and catch us a murderer or two!"

* * *

The discussion with the superintendent did not have a good effect on Burke. When he got back to his own office, he was all fired up. Fortunately, Moore and Lawler were still out of the station, otherwise they might have felt the brunt of his frustration.

When he had calmed down, he arranged for a bulletin to go out to the airports and ferry terminals with details of Freddy Taylor and Sinéad Walsh. Then he contacted a colleague in the Police Service of Northern Ireland.

"Hello, is that Inspector McClintock?"

"Yes, who's calling please?" the man said in soft northern tones.

"Hello, Sammy. It's Aidan Burke here from Dublin. How are you keeping?"

"Oh, hello, Aidan. Good, thanks. And you?"

"Fair, Sammy, only fair. Listen. I need a favour. We have two people that we're anxious to interview in connection with a couple of murders and perhaps people trafficking as well. I think they might be headed in your direction, maybe to get the ferry to Scotland, or a flight out of the country. If I send you their details, could you put the word out for us?"

"Bloody hell, Aidan. You don't do anything by halves, do you? Yes, of course. Fax through their photos and stuff, and I'll circulate it. But if they've gone by boat, it will be very hard to track them down. What names are they using?"

"Freddy Taylor and Sinéad Walsh, but they may have documents in other names too. The girl is quite striking-looking. People would notice her. And of course, they may have split up. Anyway, I appreciate your help."

"No bother, Aidan. Send up the info and I'll see what I can do."

"Thanks, Sammy. That's a wee dram I owe you."

"Ah, away with ye, Aidan. Bye for now."

People didn't realise how closely the Gardaí and the PSNI worked on a regular basis. While politically it was necessary to keep the two organisations very separate, operationally, things were different. They exchanged a great deal of information about crime and criminals that straddled the border between the two jurisdictions, and joint operations were commonplace, although they were careful not to allow officers from either force to be observed in the other's territory.

Burke asked one of the civilian clerical workers in the office to send all the information that they had on the two absconders to McClintock, and then he called Fiona Moore on her mobile.

Chapter Twenty

When Fiona Moore got back to Store Street, there were a number of messages for her. Firstly, she called Dónal Lawler to see if either of the two 'persons of interest' had been collected from their homes.

"Sorry, boss. No one in at either address. But I did get a bit of information from a neighbour a few doors down from Taylor's house. A woman was at her door at half past five this morning seeing her husband off. Apparently, he's an IT consultant, and he often travels for work. He was going to Toronto and had to be at the airport by six," Lawler said.

"So – why am I hearing the story of someone's life? What about Taylor?"

"That's just it. While she was seeing her husband off, she saw a taxi at Taylor's house, and then he came out and got into the cab. He had a suitcase with him, it seems."

"I see. I don't suppose she spotted the name of the cab company?"

"Yes, she did. She said it was the local firm, Abbey Taxis. I'm just going to call them now and get the details of the hire."

"Good man. Let me know. Thanks," Moore said.

The next call Moore made was to Sergeant Kelly, the officer in charge of Tallaght Garda Station.

"Hi, Sergeant Kelly. This is Fiona Moore. You were looking for me."

"Oh, yes, Sergeant, just hold on a second while I check something here in the book. I won't keep you."

"Thanks," Moore said, hoping he would be true to his word. She had a lot to do.

"Right, here we are," Sergeant Kelly said a few moments later, "there was a Dinny O'Leary in looking for you this morning. He didn't leave a message. He said you'd know what it was about."

"Did he leave a number?"

"No, 'fraid not. I assumed you already had it," the man said.

"I don't. But I know where he lives. I'll call out later and catch up with him. Thanks anyway," Moore said, not really meaning it.

* * *

When Burke had called Moore earlier to talk about Freddy Taylor and Sinéad Walsh, he told her he was going to apply to have their respective bank accounts frozen. It was never straightforward. Apart from the fact that the banks didn't like doing it, there always seemed to be a great deal of red tape and unnecessary administration associated with what should have been a fairly simple task. She went upstairs and spoke to the civilian worker who was assigned to the team to look after administration.

"Hi, Teresa. What's the story on the bank accounts for those two the inspector was talking to you about earlier?"

"I have been on to the banks and given them all the details. They said they will try to action it today, but that they were very busy! I ask you!"

"I hope you gave them a piece of your mind," Moore said.

"You bet. I won't repeat what I said to the girl, but suffice to say, the accounts are now frozen. She did say that Walsh had withdrawn a sizeable amount of cash early this morning though," Teresa said.

"Don't suppose she said where?"

"No. I did ask, but she just tried to blind me with science. But I gather they can't actually tell till tomorrow which ATM was used."

"Wonderful. Thanks anyway. Stay on it, will you. Oh, and Teresa, if you get time will you have a trawl through the telephone records from McCranny's office – see if anything strange jumps out at you."

"Yes, sure, boss. What am I looking for?"

"I don't know, to be honest. Just anything that seems a bit out of the ordinary. You'll know it when you see it."

"OK, will do. Thanks, boss."

Then Fiona Moore went in search of her boss. She found him in his office looking a bit grim.

"Hi. What's up? You look like you found a sixpence and lost a shilling."

"It's much worse than that, Sergeant."

"Go on."

"Ah, just the blasted Cork man has been on at me. He thinks we should have solved these two cases by now. It's easy for him, sitting on his arse in his plush office. He should try doing our job for a few days!"

"Well, anyway. What's the story?"

"Story! I wish I had a story. Our two best suspects have vanished, and I'll have to do something with that feckin' Turk downstairs too before long, or we'll have him shouting about his bloody human rights and threatening Amnesty International at us."

"Jesus, boss, take it easy. You'll burst a blood vessel. Oh, by the way, that old guy Dinny O'Leary was looking for me. Fancy a trip to the hills?"

"Maybe. What does he want?"

"I don't know, but it might be better than sitting around here spinning our wheels anyway," Moore said.

"OK. Can we take yours? I need a drink."

* * *

When they got well out of town, Burke asked Moore to stop at the Jobstown House. They went inside, and Burke ordered a pint of Guinness with a whiskey chaser, while Moore settled for a coffee.

When they were seated in a quiet part of the lounge, Burke took a mouthful of his pint, and said, "Well, what's the craic?"

"Unless Dinny comes up with something today, boss, we're buggered. Dónal has been through all the stuff they recovered from McCranny's office, and there's nothing. Not in the form of a bottle of poison and a loaded syringe in any case. He may get some use out of the financial records, if we can make head or tail of them."

"What about the other girl, Melissa? Can she tell us anything?"

"Unless she's an extremely good actor, she doesn't appear to know much. I don't think she's in on whatever is going on, but I could be wrong."

Burke coiffed half of his pint in one go this time.

"So, what's the plan, boss?" Moore said.

"Let's see what Dinny has to say, and then I'd better get back and sort out Bilal. I suppose we'll have to hand him over to the immigration folks, but not before he has identified Taylor as Mr Freddy. I want to get Taylor's and Walsh's bank accounts analysed too. You know what the Super always says – follow the money."

"Right. Well, it's getting dark now. Dinny will be coming home from the plantation. Finish up your drink and let's go."

"Yes, ma'am!" Burke said and did what he was told.

* * *

It was indeed getting dark as Burke and Moore drove on up towards the hills. Thick grey clouds which were full of rain obscured the setting sun. They saw Dinny's old green van parked at the side of the road outside his house, so Moore stopped behind it and they went to the front door.

Dinny O'Leary answered the door promptly. He was still dressed in his work clothes, and had some small twigs and pieces of pine needles lodged in his thinning hair.

"Hello, officers. You didn't have to come all the way out here. A phone call would have done." He stood back from the door. "But now that you're here, come in. Would you like a cup of tea? I've just put the kettle on."

"No, thanks, Mr O'Leary, we're fine."

Burke and Moore went inside, and when they were invited to sit, they made themselves comfortable on the wooden kitchen chairs around the small table.

"So, what's on your mind, Mr O'Leary?" Moore asked.

"Call me Dinny, Sergeant. Everyone does. I just wanted to have a chat with you about Paddy Dunne. You know the other man that works with me in the forestry."

"Yes, I know who you mean. I called to his house a couple of times, but never managed to catch him at home," Moore said.

"Aye, he told me about that, and someone searching the place and all. But here's what I'll tell you. He's a troubled soul," O'Leary said, taking a mouthful of tea from his big blue striped mug.

"What's on his mind?" Burke asked.

"We were having a chat the other day. There was just the two of us in one of the workmen's huts up amongst the trees, and we were having a bit of lunch. He was telling me that he had seen the two men in the BMW on the day that all this happened."

"I see. Did he say any more?"

"Oh, he did all right. He said he saw the car parked in an unusual spot down by a place we call Foxes Grove. He passed by the car, and he could see there were two men in it, and he said they were doing some unnatural things. Disgusted he was. He didn't elaborate, but I'm sure you can imagine. Now don't get me wrong. We get a good few courting couples up here, especially in the winter when it's quiet. And I know some of them get up to all sorts because they've nowhere else to go. But Paddy said this was different. Two men – he said. It's just not right."

"And did he say anything more, Dinny?" Moore asked.

"He did. I could tell he was fierce upset about it all, so I drew him out a bit. He told me that he had done something terrible after that. It was on his conscience, but he couldn't help himself."

"Did he say what exactly this terrible thing was, Dinny?" Burke asked.

"No. No, he didn't, and I'm not one to speculate. But with the two men ending up dead – well, I'm sure you can figure out what's going through my head."

"OK, Dinny. Thanks for your help. Not a word to Paddy now. We'll be talking to him as soon as we can, but if you bump into him in the meantime, say nothing, OK?" Burke said.

"Yes, of course. But I'll not see him till we get to work tomorrow morning. And don't you two go telling him what I've told you either, do you hear?"

"It's OK, Dinny. We won't let on."

The two detectives left Dinny's house and sat into Moore's car outside.

"Shall we go and have a word?" Burke said.

"Listen, boss, I have a night class to go to in town. It starts at seven, and I don't want to miss it. Could we leave Dunne till the morning? I can arrange for a few men from Tallaght to come and lift him around half past six and bring him into town for us," Moore said.

"Good idea, Fiona, I could do with getting home myself. I guess that would work. He's hardly likely to abscond overnight. Right – let's go back to town then."

Chapter Twenty-One

Moore arrived at the night class just after seven. It was being held in the community centre near her home, and there were three men and five other women on the course. The tutor was a very experienced photographer who had won many awards for his work over the years, but still managed to remain humble, and very helpful to his novice charges.

They started the class with the instructor having a look at the photographs that the students had taken since their last class. Moore readied her Nikon, and scrolled through the pictures, several of which were taken inside Paddy Dunne's house. As she did so, examining each frame in detail, her heart stopped. In one of the pictures, standing on the draining board amid loads of rubbish, dirty dishes and discarded food cartons there was a mug, and it looked very much like there was the top of a hypodermic syringe sticking up out of it.

Moore excused herself from the class and went outside to call Burke. She told him what she had discovered, and asked that he inform the Tallaght lads that were going to pay a house call on Paddy Dunne early the following morning to collect the item under the aegis of the warrant that had been issued a few days previously, that was still in force.

"How did you miss that when you were collecting the knife?" Burke said.

"I don't know, boss. I guess I was so focused on getting the blade, I didn't really pay much attention to anything else. And the place was in such a state, I just didn't see it."

"OK. Well, no harm done. Let's just hope it's still in situ tomorrow morning. If we do get hold of it, get it over to the lab and get them working on it. Thank God for your camera classes!" Burke said.

"I'd better get back in. See you tomorrow."

When she returned to the class, the instructor took Fiona's camera in his hands and scrolled through the images.

"These are very good, Fiona. You've captured the mood of the old place very nicely. You've used available light to good effect. And they are all in focus – well, nearly all. The background in two or three of them is nicely blurred – we call that the Bokeh effect, and you get it by opening up the lens to its maximum aperture – probably f1.8 in this case. Very nice."

"Yes, that's the look I was hoping for," she lied. Little did he know.

* * *

It was a bitterly cold and damp morning when the squad car from Tallaght pulled up outside Paddy Dunne's broken-down cottage in the dark.

"This is a right bloody caper," the burly Garda who was driving said. "You'd think they could do their own dirty work," he said opening the door and clambering out into the freezing early morning air.

"Are ye coming?" he said, leaning back into the vehicle addressing the pretty young brunette who had been assigned to accompany him.

"Right with you, Cormac. Is it cold out there?" she said, still not opening the door of the white Hyundai.

"C'mon, Gráinne, will ye stop messing."

The girl smiled as she got out of the car and fixed her Garda cap over her shiny brown hair.

They advanced carefully up the path towards the house, using their Maglite torches to avoid getting snagged on the rubbish that festooned the little patch of overgrown grass and weeds. Cormac rapped hard three times on the decrepit old front door with such force that it opened a few centimetres all by itself.

Cormac looked at the girl, who just shrugged. Cormac pushed the door open. It creaked and scraped across the stoop, revealing the dark inside of the little house, and allowing some of the rancid smell to waft out as far as the two Gardaí. He shone the torch inside, illuminating the dirty kitchen, and then gingerly, they entered the house.

They found Paddy Dunne asleep in his bedroom. The room was just as dirty and disorganised as the rest of the dwelling. Paddy was beginning to stir, and when he threw back the dirty old eiderdown that had been keeping him warm, the two Gardaí observed that he was still, largely, dressed.

"Who the hell are you?" he exclaimed trying to shield his eyes from the brightness of Cormac's torch.

"We're the police, Mr Dunne. You'll need to get up and come with us. Come along now," the Garda instructed.

"What? What are you talking about? It's the middle of the night. Leave me alone." He turned over presenting his back to the officer, and pulling the bed clothes up around him once again.

Sensing that her colleague was in no danger from the old guy, the female officer went back into the kitchen. She found the mug with the syringe in it exactly where Inspector Burke had said it would be, and she lifted it, using a piece of paper, by the very tip of the plunger, and dropped it into an evidence bag, noting that it had a needle attached.

Cormac emerged from the bedroom escorting a very sleepy and reluctant Paddy Dunne with him. Paddy was muttering about police harassment under his breath, but it was nothing that the Gardaí were not used to.

The unlikely trio made their way back to the Garda car. The female officer placed the hypodermic in a box fixed to the boot floor of their car, and then sat in beside the fragrant old man in the back seat, while Cormac set off for Store Street.

When they got to town, Paddy was brought before the desk sergeant who was just finishing his shift, and anxious to get away while the city traffic was still manageable, took his details and escorted him to a cell.

* * *

When the night man in Store Street had handed over his shift, and the hour had become decent, the sergeant called Burke on his mobile phone to advise him that they had Paddy Dunne in custody.

"What do you want me to do with him, Inspector?" the sergeant said.

"Any chance you could rustle him up a spot of breakfast – maybe a breakfast roll from the café across the road. Make him feel at home."

"I'll just see if we have any silver plates and fine bone china cups here to serve it on, shall I? I'm sure that's what he's used to, given the state of him."

"Whatever, Sergeant. Thanks."

The sergeant put the phone down and muttered, "Blooming cheek!" to himself, before summoning a young trainee Garda and giving him instructions.

When Paddy got his breakfast, accompanied by a large mug of strong, hot tea, he surveyed his surroundings. Although he was incarcerated, he had to admit that the cell he was in, with its little stainless toilet and hand basin, good supply of toilet paper and paper towels and quite a comfortable blue mattress, was a considerable improvement on his own place. And the food was pretty good too. He wouldn't mind spending a few days in here at all, although he knew that the novelty would soon wear off, and he would long for the wide-open spaces and solitude of the Dublin Mountains. But for now, it would do nicely. He knew what the Gardaí wanted. But he'd see if he could string it out for a while so that he could take full advantage of their hospitality.

* * *

Moore arrived in the station a few minutes before her boss and went to talk to Dónal Lawler who was already at work.

"Hi, Dónal. Any word on Taylor and Walsh?"

"No, boss. Not a sign. They seem to have vanished into thin air."

"Have you checked to see if their phones have been turned back on? What about any more ATM withdrawals?"

"Negative on both, boss."

"So, what are you up to?"

"I have a girl coming down from the Park to go through the accounts and stuff we brought back from McCranny's office. She's a civilian worker – an accountant – attached to the Fraud Squad. We're going to see if we can track where these payments into McCranny's accounts have been coming from. You know, follow the money as it were."

"Good idea. Let me know if you find anything interesting."

Burke got to the station a short while later, and called Moore into his office.

"Right, what have we got, Fiona?"

"We have the old timer from the woods downstairs. And the syringe has gone to the lab for analysis. That's about it."

"OK. What do you think yourself?"

"Well, it's certainly a coincidence, and you know what I think about those. But it's hard to see how Paddy could have administered the poison. He hardly had access to McCranny's smokes. Let's see what the lab says. What about Bilal?"

"Oh, shit, yeah. I'd better see what we can do with him. Get me a photo of Freddy Taylor from somewhere, will you, and I'll see if he can identify him."

"Give me a few minutes," Moore said.

She went back to the open plan and logged into her PC. She tried LinkedIn, but there was, surprisingly, no sign of an architect called Freddy Taylor on the site.

Then she tried Facebook, but still no joy.

"Hmm, interesting," she said to herself.

Then she brought up a deep search engine used by police forces across Europe and put in his name. The system displayed the egg-timer for quite a while, but finally showed three lines with links to a number of other sites referencing Freddy Taylor.

One of the links connected Moore through to the Bolton Street College of Technology Alumni. There, listed as a benefactor to the College was the man himself, complete with what looked like a fairly recent photograph.

"That'll do me!" Moore said to no one in particular, and she fired up the printer and sent the picture to it.

Chapter Twenty-Two

"Well, Bilal. We have a photograph for you to have a look at," Burke said, turning the printed page that Moore had downloaded around so he could see it. But Bilal didn't look down at the photograph. Instead, he looked directly into Burke's eyes and said, "Inspector, before I help you with this, I need to know that you are going to carry out your promise to help me and my family. They will already be wondering why I don't send any money this week. They will not have food to eat."

Burke thought for a moment.

"I'll tell you what I will do, Bilal. Give me the details of where you send your money, and I will personally send €100 off today to your family. This will show you that I meant what I said about helping you."

"You would do that? Send money to my Aisha?"

"Yes. Is Aisha your wife?"

"Yes, she is. Give me paper. I will write down the account details," Bilal said. He was hardly able to believe what the policeman had said to him. This was not the way the police operated where he came from. He wondered if it might be some sort of trick, but the thought of his beautiful wife and wonderful children starving, and not having any money to buy food, overcame his misgivings.

Burke gave Bilal a sheet from his jotter and a pen, and the man wrote down some numbers along with the name Aisha Demir.

"That is the account name, and those are the numbers you will need. When will you send the money?"

"Just as soon as you identify the man in the photograph, Bilal."

Demir looked down at the photograph and smiled.

"That is Mr Freddy. It's funny."

"Why do you say that?"

"Because he is never looking as good as this picture when he comes to our lodgings, but it is definitely him."

"And can you confirm that this man comes to the yard every week and pays you and your fellow workmen in cash for the work you have done?" Burke said.

"Yes. Cash. Every week."

"Right, thanks, Bilal. Now I'll go and arrange the payment to your wife."

"When will I get out of here, Inspector? If I am not working, I will not make any money to send home."

"Not for a few days, Bilal. And it may not be possible for you to work for a little while. We'll have to see how things go. Right now, I need to find your Mr Freddy."

Bilal slumped back in the chair looking a bit dejected, and folded his arms across his chest.

* * *

Burke handed the piece of paper with the account details to Fiona Moore.

"Here, we need to send €100 to this account. But much more importantly, we need to find out exactly where the account is held. I want the bank name, street address, town or city and the address of the account holder. Can you organise that?"

"I'm sure I can, boss, yes."

"And while you're at it, do a deep search for Aisha Demir as well, and see if anything comes up."

Moore felt like giving a little curtsey, but managed to restrain herself. She turned around to go and do his bidding, but Burke called her back.

"Oh, Fiona, do you think you could do the interview with Paddy Dunne? The boss wants me upstairs, and anyway, I think Dunne might respond better to a female officer."

"Yes, OK, if you think that's the way it is," Moore said.

"I do. Thanks," Burke said.

Moore walked off back to her desk, muttering under her breath, "If you stick a brush up my arse, I'll sweep up the place as I run around after you too."

Back at her desk, Moore deciphered the codes on the slip of paper Bilal Demir had written down using a bank look-up application on her PC. The bank was in a town called Reyhanli, in southern Turkey, very close to the Syrian border. The town had a population of almost 100,000, and had been in the past subjected to some terrorist activity, but not, according to reports, recently. The bank that the money was to go to was called Halkbank, and seemed to be a perfectly normal commercial undertaking.

Moore looked up the bank on the web. Helpfully, the bank's website gave a full address and even a telephone number for the establishment, but it seemed that it was closed at that hour, and would open again the next day at nine in the morning. Moore was surprised to find that the town was three hours ahead of the time in Dublin, something she simply hadn't thought of.

But there was still time to get to the local bank before it closed. Moore put on her coat, took the details of Bilal's bank with her and left the office. She crossed the road and went to a branch where she was known. She queued up at the Foreign Exchange window, and waited patiently while the customer in front of her negotiated the purchase of several hundred dollars. Eventually, the man seemed satisfied, but not before he had regaled the bank clerk with every possible detail about his daughter who lived in Upstate New York with her hardworking husband and two children.

Then it was Moore's turn.

"Hello, Christine. I need to send one hundred euro to an account in Turkey," she said, presenting the slip of paper with the Turkish bank's details on it.

"Let me see," Christine said. She rummaged under the counter and brought out a slim, well-thumbed booklet, and turned the pages, muttering, "Turkey, Turkey," under her breath.

"Yes, here we are. Oh, unfortunately the bank you have given me is not our correspondent bank in Turkey, so it will have to go first to another bank, and then be transferred internally to Halkbank. It could take a few days. Is that OK?" Christine asked.

"I guess so. What will it cost to send the money?"

"Let's see. I'm afraid it will be twenty-two euro. Do you want to pay that separately, or take it out of the €100?"

"Cripes! Just for sending a fax or a telex or something? That seems quite steep," Moore said.

"Hold on a sec. I might be able to use staff rates. That would bring it down to eight euro. Is that better?"

"Yes, a lot. Thanks. I'll pay that on top of the €100 then."

Moore completed the transaction, got a receipt for the charges as well as confirmation that the money had been sent, and left the bank.

She went back to the Garda station, stopping at Costa Coffee for an Americano on the way. She needed it to get her ready for the interview with Paddy Dunne.

Back at the station, she checked to see if there was any news back from forensics concerning the contents of the syringe that they had removed from Paddy's house, but there was nothing as yet.

* * *

Paddy Dunne was still enjoying the relative comfort of the police station cell. He had been given a good lunch comprised of piping hot mushroom soup and a whopper of a chicken sandwich, all rounded off with a cup of tea and two chocolate biscuits. He hadn't eaten so well in years. The desk sergeant had even left him a copy of the Irish Independent to read, so when he was collected to go to the interview room, he was both replete and relaxed.

"Well, Paddy. I hope they are looking after you OK now?" Moore said to the man as she sat down opposite him in the interview room. A uniformed Garda was also present, standing with his legs apart and hands behind his back close to the door.

"Oh, they are, to be sure. I can't complain. How's yourself?"

"I need to ask you some questions about what happened up near the woods the other day. You remember – the thing with the young lad that was found in the hut?"

"Oh, that. Terrible business. I got an awful fright, you know," Paddy said.

"Yes, well, we all did. But we are here, Paddy, because we found a hypodermic syringe in your kitchen. Can you tell me what that was doing there?"

"Someone must have put it there. I never had anything to do with them things. I'm not that tidy about the house, so I might not have noticed."

"Are you sure, now, Paddy? It's important. Try and remember."

Paddy scratched his head and looked down at his boots for a minute.

"Oh, wait a second. A syringe you say? Yes, yes, now I remember." He laughed briefly to himself.

"I had a bit of woodworm in the kitchen table, and it even got into one or two of the chairs. Someone told me that if I got one of them things and injected the holes with woodworm killer, that would do the trick. I must have left it lying around."

"I see. Tell me Paddy, do you smoke?"

"Smoke? Me? No, I never. Ah, I might have had the odd puff around the back of the bike shed at school, but I never liked it. No, I don't smoke. Why do you ask?"

"So, there wouldn't be any tobacco products anywhere in your house then?"

"No, I told you."

"And are you sure you never saw the young lad before?" Moore said.

"Before what?"

"Before he was found naked and dead in the workmen's hut."

Again, Paddy scratched his head. He looked away, and it was clear to Moore that he was very uneasy. Then, looking sideways at Moore said, "No, of course not."

"OK, Paddy. Look, we have some more enquiries to make. You'll be fine here for a while longer. I'll get them to organise a nice tea for you. We might have to keep you here overnight."

"That's no bother. I'm grand and cosy where I am."

Chapter Twenty-Three

When Moore got back to her desk, there was a message for her to call forensics. Brian Bradley answered the phone, and Moore said that she was returning a call.

"Yes, yes, now where is it," Bradley said. "Here we are – Cuprinol."

"Cuprinol? What about it?"

"The syringe that was brought in earlier. It contains a few drops of Cuprinol. It's pretty old too. Most of it had evaporated."

"Go on, make my day. Tell me it's a source of arsenic."

Bradley laughed down the phone.

"No, it's nothing like that. It's an insecticide. Often used to kill woodworm in old furniture. I've seen quite a few people use it in a needle like that. It's the only way you can get the stuff into the holes they make and snuff the little buggers out."

"Shit! And there's no other substance present?"

"No. It's neat Cuprinol."

"What about fingerprints?"

"There's a nice neat thumb print on the top of the plunger that matches to the owner of the property – Dunne, is it?"

"Yes, Paddy Dunne. OK, thanks, Brian. Or should I say, no thanks."

"Sorry, Sarge."

Moore went in search of Aidan Burke whom she found in his office. She brought him up to speed on what she had discovered from forensics.

"Maybe I should have a go at Paddy Dunne. Everyone here is treating him like some kind of VIP. Maybe he needs more robust questioning. I'll go down in a few minutes and give him a proper grilling. Did you get the money away to Turkey?"

"Yes, I did. Bloody robbers – wanted to charge me twenty euro to send it. But I got it down to eight. I have the details of the bank account back at my desk," Moore said.

"Right, well when I'm down chatting to the woodsman, will you try and get on to the Turkish cops in Reyhanli, or whatever it's called, and see what they have on the Demirs?"

"Yes, OK. Any word on the elusive architect?"

"No, nothing. We have a good watch set up on all the ports and airports. They can't have got away."

"Don't bet on it. Don't forget these two are experts in people smuggling. I can't quite see them hunkered down in the back of a forty-foot trailer, but you never know. Have we got alerts set up for any activity on the bank cards?" Burke said.

"Yes, of course. But given the time of year, it could be a day or two before the banks notify us."

"Not good enough. Get that escalated – straight away. And why don't you see if there's any news of the Sprinter Transport van too?"

"OK, boss. I'll get on it now."

When Moore had left, Burke went off to interview Paddy Dunne.

Paddy Dunne was just finishing his mug of tea when the sergeant came in to bring him back to the interview room.

"God, 'tis fierce busy here today. Who is looking for the pleasure of my company now? I hope it's that bonnie lass, Moore," he said.

"You're out of luck, Paddy. It's the boss, Inspector Burke, and I never heard him described as bonnie, that's for sure!"

Burke was in the room when Paddy Dunne was brought in. Paddy could feel the difference in the attitude straight away. Gone was the affable banter. This man was serious about his work, Dunne calculated. Maybe he needed to tell the truth this time.

* * *

Moore set about the tasks that Burke had given her. When she had called the security department in the three main banks to escalate the alert if either Taylor or Walsh used their card, she put out a shout for any sightings of the Sprinter Transport van. She attached a 'code red' to the message that would go to every Garda station in the land, in the hope that someone had seen it, or it had been caught on CCTV somewhere.

Then she turned her attention to Turkey. Although Turkey was not a member of the European Union, there was an 'Agreement of Cooperation' in place between the country and Europol, just as Europol had with countries like Israel and even Japan. Depending on the issue involved, that agreement often provided much the same degree of assistance that was enjoyed by full members. Basic criminal activity, such as the drug trade, people trafficking, kidnap, blackmail, murder and manslaughter was all managed in a spirit of full cooperation, while more politically sensitive matters enjoyed a slightly lower priority.

Moore decided to start with the Turkish police headquarters in Ankara. The force's website, helpfully, provided a telephone number, and Moore called it at once, anxious not to get caught out by the three-hour time difference again.

It took some time, but after a few false starts, and discovering that very few of the staff spoke English, Moore got through to Sub-Inspector Galip Avci. Avci spoke quite good English, and he immediately put Moore at her ease by requesting that they deal on first name terms to avoid unnecessary formality.

"Thanks, Galip, that does make things easier," Moore said, warming to the man.

"What can I do for you this evening, Fiona?" he said.

Moore explained the Garda's interest in Bilal Demir and his wife. She provided all the detail that they held on the couple, explaining that they appear to have lived, or be living in Reyhanli.

"This is a very troubled area, Fiona. Since the war in Syria, there has been a lot of disruption all around there. I'm not surprised this Bilal wanted to get away. But I'm afraid our computer systems are not as advanced as you may have in Ireland. I will have to contact a colleague in Reyhanli to enquire about the Demirs. Would it be all right if I called you back, maybe tomorrow?" Avci said.

"Yes, of course, that would be great." Moore then gave the man her contact details, including her email address and mobile phone number in case he wanted to contact her out of hours.

* * *

"Right, Mr Dunne. Now, I want you to tell me all you know about the death of Felix Lahart in the woods where you work. And don't piss me about. You wouldn't like me when I'm angry!" Burke said.

Paddy Dunne thought for a moment, scratched his head, and said, "I suppose I better tell you the whole thing. You'll find out anyway."

"Go on," Burke said.

"I was out for a walk that evening. It was a fine afternoon, although it was cold. But the air up there is grand, and I enjoy a walk. I first saw the car parked in off the road, and I was a bit puzzled, because what with the temperature and all, it wasn't the time for courting couples. But as I came up alongside it from behind, I could see there were two men in the car. Then, when I was right beside the driver's door, I could see in. God it was disgusting. That young fella had his head down in the driver's lap, and yer man had his pants open, and they were… well, you know. It's not natural that sort of thing. And it made me angry, but what could I do? So, I just walked on up the road, feeling more and more angry with each step."

Dunne stopped his story, and took a sip from the glass of water that had been left on the table.

"And were they both alive and well when you had finished gawking in the window?"

"Hold your whisht now, Inspector. I haven't finished."

Burke said nothing, allowing Dunne to continue his tale.

"I walked on up to the top of that road, just to where it levels out and gives you a great view of the city. It would have taken me about forty minutes. Then I turned around and started back down heading for home. I came across the car, gone off the road and crashed into the tree. There was no sign of the young lad, but the driver was still inside slumped over the steering wheel. I didn't know if he was dead or alive, but I thought to myself that he had got what was coming to him."

"You didn't touch anything – like the car door, or the man inside?"

"No, not at all. But I was curious about where the young fella had made off to," Dunne said.

"So, what about the young lad?" Burke asked.

"I know those woods like the back of my hand. I knew if he had done a runner, where he would end up. There's nowhere else to go up around there. He had to be in the old hut. So, I went in after him. My blood was fair boiling by that time. I got to the hut, and there he was inside trying to fix himself up a bit after the crash. I just saw red. I had a good strong knife with me – I always carry one when I'm out in the forest in case I come across a trapped animal or something – so I crept up on the lad and knifed him, didn't I?"

"Jesus, Paddy. You must have been mad!"

"God, I was fierce riled up. That's when I carved the letters on him using a sharp piece of stick, the dirty little fecker. It isn't right, you know. Not natural."

"Did you know that you had killed him?"

"I didn't care by that time. I just took his clothes away and set off back for home."

"What did you do with the clothes?" Burke said.

"I burnt them at home. He wasn't wearing much anyway. I suppose he didn't expect to find himself out in the open on a day like that. God, I'm very sorry, Inspector. I don't know what came over me. The devil took a hold of me."

"I wouldn't rely too heavily on that defence, if I were you."

Despite what Paddy Dunne had said, Burke couldn't help but feel a bit of empathy for the old guy. He was a loner who had grown up in the fifties and sixties in Ireland when the country was dominated by the Catholic Church. Homosexuality was not only illegal, but was also an abhorrence to much of the population at large, sentiments preached regularly by Catholic priests from the pulpit at Mass. It wasn't until 1993 that it was finally decriminalised, following a campaign by Senator David Norris, and a ruling five years earlier by the European Courts that Irish Law was in contravention of the European Convention on Human Rights.

Homosexuality didn't prove to be the pariah that everyone had feared. The LGBT community quickly became well integrated into Irish society, and were very largely accepted by all but a few traditionalists that clung to the outdated and illiberal teachings of the 1950s. The LGBT cause had been greatly helped by the fall from grace of the Catholic Church itself, which had become embroiled in several controversies involving paedophilia.

But murder was murder, and Paddy's old-fashioned beliefs were no excuse for it.

"Look, I'm going to charge you with murder for now, Paddy. Legal representation will be appointed for you. It's a bad business. You'll get a good long sentence too, believe me," Burke said.

"Ah, sure, won't I be fed and watered and kept warm and dry inside? It won't be that bad. I'll survive."

Burke escorted the old man back to the front desk where he formally charged him with murder in front of the desk sergeant. A more detailed statement would be taken from him at a later point. He would appear in court the following day, and Burke told him the Gardaí wouldn't oppose bail.

When the formalities had been cleared up, Burke went upstairs to report to Heffernan that they had solved one of the murders in this complex case.

Chapter Twenty-Four

While Burke was dealing with Paddy Dunne, Moore's thoughts had turned to the death of Gerald McCranny. The way he had been killed involved quite a sophisticated process. Assuming it was arsenic poisoning, and not the crash that had seen him off, Moore wondered how, and more importantly, who, could have perpetrated the crime. Instinctively, she would have jumped at the wife as being the killer. Although they lived what appeared to be quite separate lives, and Mrs McCranny seemed on the surface of things to be quite content, nine times out of ten, cases of this kind are usually down to a close family member.

But if his wife had been involved, where was the poison obtained? Moore had heard that arsenic could be extracted quite easily in a laboratory, but that's hardly the kind of thing you could do at home – at least not without being discovered.

Moore turned to her PC and Googled 'where can I buy arsenic?'. The search engine revealed several links, and after a short time browsing, Moore discovered that it was very possible to buy the product online. If you got hold of white arsenic – the powder form – it could be easily dissolved in water and injected.

"Wow! There's a surprise. I think I need another word with Mrs McCranny!" she said to herself.

Before calling the woman to see if she was in, Moore spoke to Dónal Lawler.

"Dónal, do we have any information on Gerald McCranny's personal bank accounts – you know, did they have a joint account; joint credit cards, that sort of thing?"

"I'm not sure, Sarge. Want me to have a root around?"

"Yes, please. I'm going out for a while, but phone anything you find through to me, will you?"

"Sure. What exactly are we looking for?"

"I want to see if she made any online purchases of any chemicals. You'll probably have to do quite a bit of research, but look for a PayPal or card transaction for around twenty US dollars, or thereabouts. And it would have been done a few weeks before McCranny died. If you find anything that looks right, dig deeper. I'd like to know what it was for and who the supplier is. OK?"

"Yes, no worries. See you later."

Moore then called the McCranny household and spoke to Janine.

"Hello, Sergeant. Yes, I think Mrs McCranny will be in until later, but hold on a minute, I'll go and check."

Moore could hear the clip-clop of the girl's shoes on the tiled hallway over the phone as she went to find her boss, and a minute later, the footsteps once again approaching.

"Yes, Sergeant, Mrs McCranny will be here till late afternoon, if you want to call."

"Great, thanks, Janine. I'll be there in about forty minutes."

Traffic was relatively light at that hour of the day, and once Moore had left the city centre, she made good time on the Stillorgan Road taking her to Foxrock. Thirty-five minutes after leaving the Garda station, she was ringing the bell at McCranny's house, waiting for the familiar sound of Janine's footsteps on the hallway.

Janine showed Moore into the sumptuous sitting room where she had been before. She noted that the house had an easy, relaxed feeling about it – not at all the usual scenario for a home that had just lost its patriarch. As she waited, Moore admired some of the paintings that adorned the walls. She was particularly drawn to a landscape of the west of Ireland, featuring a small group of fishermen attending to a currach. The men were dressed in tweed suits and tweed caps, which Moore recognised as being typical of the kind of outfits such men would have worn in the late nineteenth century.

"That's by Maurice Wilks. Do you like it?" a voice behind Moore said.

Turning, she saw that it was Mrs McCranny, so she shook hands with the woman before returning to admire the artwork.

"Yes, I do. It's very evocative of the area, and the period."

"It is. Gerald bought it for me several years ago as an anniversary present. I think it's worth quite a bit these days. Anyway, what can I do for you today, Sergeant?"

The two women took their seats on the comfortable chairs facing each other at the fireside. The fire wasn't lit, but the room was warm despite the weather outside.

"Mrs McCranny, did Gerald and yourself have any joint banking arrangements – such as a joint account?"

"No, not recently. We did have when we were married first, but when Gerald got heavily involved in construction, he said it would be better to keep our affairs separate, so I have my own account."

"What about credit cards? Are they separate too?" Moore said.

"Yes, of course. You should know, Sergeant, that I have my own income from the company. I also have an annuity that my father left me. I have as much money as I need."

"Well, that's good anyway. I wonder if you would object if we took a copy of your bank and credit card statements?"

The woman looked puzzled.

"Well, I don't see the relevance, Sergeant, but if it will help catch Gerald's killer, then I suppose so. I keep copies upstairs. I know they want us to be all electronic these days, but I prefer the old-fashioned methods. How far do you want to go back?"

"Six months would be terrific, if that's not too much trouble?"

"No, that's all right. I'll just go and get them for you. Would you like some tea while you are waiting?"

"Thanks. That would be lovely," Moore said.

The woman departed and Moore took the chance to call Dónal Lawler on her mobile phone. She told him not to pursue Mrs McCranny's bank account details until she got back to the station.

Just as she was finishing the call, Janine arrived into the sitting room with a tray. There was a large bone china teapot, two matching cups and saucers, a milk jug, a sugar bowl with sugar lumps and silver tongs, and a plate of biscuits.

"Shall I pour your tea, officer?" Janine asked.

"No, it's fine thanks, I can manage. Thank you very much."

Moore carefully poured herself a cup of tea, helped herself to two biscuits, and sat back in her chair.

"I could get used to this," she said to herself.

Mrs McCranny came back into the room carrying three separate sheaves of paper, each one held together with a small coloured fold-back clip.

As she sat down, she offered the paperwork to Moore.

"Here you go. I've separated them into the three accounts. The top one is my current account. The next one is my credit card, and the last one is my investment account. There's hardly any movement on that one, so there's just two pages. What are you hoping to find?"

"We're not sure. The boss just wants to have a complete picture about everything. Your husband's accounts are quite complex. He had several companies, as you know, and they seem to be quite interconnected. So, this will help us to decipher what's what. I'll keep them safely for you, don't worry."

"I have no idea what he was up to in business. He just gave me some papers to sign from time to time. But he never left me short. He was a good provider."

Moore looked for some sign of compassion towards the woman's dead husband in her eyes, but could detect none. Funny how some people live their lives, she thought to herself.

"Well, thank you very much for your help, Mrs McCranny. I'd better be getting back to town. We'll keep you informed if there are any developments. How's your daughter bearing up?"

As the two women walked to the front door, Mrs McCranny said, "Oh, she's fine – as much as can be expected. She wasn't close to her father. In fact, I think she was a bit disgusted with his carry on."

"Did she know about his lifestyle then?"

"Yes, it looks like she did. She was very upset when she found out at first. But then she turned against him, and would have nothing to do with him. To be honest, I don't think she will miss him at all."

Chapter Twenty-Five

When Moore got back, she gave the statements to Lawler, asking him to use them to continue the research she had asked for earlier. Lawler told her that Inspector Burke was looking for her.

"He's charged Paddy Dunne with the murder of Felix Lahart. Seems he got a confession out of him," Lawler said.

"Wow! Nice one. That must have put him in a good humour."

"Don't bet on it, boss."

She found Burke smouldering quietly in his office, tapping his pen on the desk.

"Where have you been?" he said.

"Nice to see you too, sir. I was out visiting Mrs McCranny as you suggested."

"Well?"

"Nothing we didn't already know. I hear you got a confession out of Paddy Dunne."

Burke's phone rang before he got a chance to reply.

"Is that Inspector Burke?" the man with a country accent said at the other end of the line.

"Yes. Who's calling please?"

"Oh, thank God. It's taken me ages to get through to you. My name is Cathal Devlin, and I work down here at the ferry terminal. I think you're making enquiries about a Ford Transit belonging to Sprinter Transport. Would that be right?"

Burke looked at Moore and beckoned her to sit down.

"Yes, that's right. What's the story?"

"Well, it came through here about an hour and a half ago. There was the driver and a good-looking young lassie with him, and they got on board the ferry," Devlin said.

"I see. Can you hold them for us? Make up some story about the vehicle being unsafe or something."

"Ah, well, I could. But you see the ferry has already sailed. It's about twelve miles offshore by now, so I'm afraid they're gone."

"Christ! Where is the ferry bound for?" Burke demanded.

"Cherbourg – that's in France."

"Why the hell didn't you call us earlier, Mr Devlin?"

"Sure, it gets fierce busy here when there's a ship to load and unload. And if it doesn't sail on time, there's all hell to pay. And anyway, I've been holding on to get through to you for at least twenty minutes. I must have spoken to every Garda in Dublin!"

"OK, OK. Take it easy. When does the ship arrive in Cherbourg?"

"That would be around eleven o'clock tomorrow morning, depending on the sea state, it could be half an hour either way," Devlin said.

"And do you have a name for the occupants of the van?"

"I do, surely. Mr and Mrs O'Brien."

"Right. Well, thanks for the call anyway. We'll get onto it right away."

"What do you want them for anyway?" Devlin said, the man's natural curiosity coming into play.

"You wouldn't believe me if I told you, Mr Devlin. I'd better get on. Thanks."

When the call was over, Burke asked Moore, "Did you get all of that?"

"Yes, I did. What in God's name do we do now?"

"Go and find out what the flight situation is that will get us to France, Cherbourg, ahead of that ferry. I'll see if I can square something with Heffernan for us to lift them without causing an international incident. We don't have time to get a Europol warrant."

"OK. I'm on it."

* * *

"Blimey, Aidan, are you serious?" Heffernan said.

"Yes, boss, totally. We think these two may have been responsible for the murder of Gerald McCranny, and we know they're into people trafficking too – or at least one of them is. It's pretty heavy stuff," Burke said.

"I see. Well, you might just be in luck. I was at a conference in the Netherlands last year on combatting international terrorism, and I met a man from the French anti-terror police and we got on well. He introduced me to some very fine wines over dinner. I suppose I could give him a call. What do you want to do?"

"We want to get to France before the ferry docks, and lift them when they arrive, sir."

"You don't do things by halves, do you Burke? And how are you planning to get there ahead of the ferry, might I ask?"

"We're going to fly over, if we can get suitable flights. Sergeant Moore is sorting that out now."

"Give me half an hour, and I'll find you," Heffernan said.

* * *

Moore was having no luck. At this time of year, the nearest they could get to Cherbourg by air was Paris, but the onward travel to Cherbourg was a nightmare. It was more than four hours by road, and in any case, they would have to hire a car and bring the suspects back across northern France to Paris and on to Dublin by air. All very tricky. The French police would need to be involved, not to mention what might happen at passport control at the airport.

Then she had an idea. She went in search of Burke, and explained what she had in mind.

"Top marks for thinking out of the box, Fiona," he said, his humour having improved now that there was actually some action taking place. "But it's a bit crazy, don't you think?"

"Well, short of teleporting ourselves across, it's the only thing that will work, as far as I can see. Shall I set it up?" Moore said.

"Let's wait till Heffernan gets back to me. He's contacting the French authorities to see what they think of us arresting two Irish suspects on their soil. I can only imagine there will be about a year's worth of paperwork involved, knowing the French."

With that, Burke's phone rang.

"Yes, sir. Thanks for getting back so quickly. What's the story?"

"I've spoken to Yves, and he says that there is a way to do this, but you may not like it. You need to board the ferry and arrest them on board. Technically, that's still Irish territory. You can't go ashore with them, so you'll have to hold them on the ferry and bring them back on it. That way, the French authorities won't be involved. And there's a *quid pro quo.*"

"What's that, sir?"

"Anything we find out about the trafficking operation – we share that intelligence with him. He says it will do him no end of good if he can bring some new information to bear on that dirty business. The French are fed up with it."

"That's no bother, sir. As soon as we have anything of value, I'll let you know," Burke said.

"Yes, bring it here before it goes out anywhere else. You know what they say – information is power!"

"Yes, of course, sir."

"Right, Fiona, you're on – set it up!"

* * *

Moore got back onto her contact in the Irish Air Corps. She had learnt that they had a machine quite capable of doing the journey from Baldonnel Airdrome to Cherbourg in just over three hours. It was an Augusta Westland AW139, which had an endurance of over five hours and 1,000 kilometres – well capable of taking the two of them to France and bringing the four of them back.

The Air Corps would need an authorisation from Superintendent Heffernan and indemnities concerning the passengers, and it was made very clear that under no circumstances were firearms to be carried on board. The flight crew would be armed with side arms, and a further deployment of two infantrymen would accompany the expedition, keeping the payload well within limits for the aircraft which was capable of transporting fifteen people.

Captain Ray O'Donnell would be the pilot, ably assisted by Flight Corporal Mairéad O'Loughlin.

"I can get the paperwork sorted today, Captain. Will there be any charge for these services?"

"I'll have a word with the Commandant, Sergeant, but I suspect we will be able to put it down as a training exercise. That will avoid any awkward questions in the Dáil if it should come under scrutiny. I need to go and prepare a flight plan now, so if that's all, we'll see you tomorrow morning at 6:30 Zulu for a 7:00 a.m. departure. OK?" O'Donnell said.

"Yes, super. Many thanks, Captain."

Moore went and relayed the information to Burke, who said he wasn't looking forward to getting Heffernan to approve this little caper.

"Still, it's the only thing that works, but it's très dodgy if you ask me."

Chapter Twenty-Six

"How did Heffernan take it?" Moore asked when she collected Aidan Burke at his home in Crumlin at six o'clock the following morning.

"He nearly had a conniption. But he got back onto his pal, Yves, who apparently thought it was a brilliant idea, so he was happier then. They agreed a variation on the plan too."

"Oh – what's that then?" Moore said.

"I'll tell you later. Looks like a nice morning for it. Have you been in a helicopter before?"

"Yes, but not for a long journey like this. I was up over Alcatraz one time when we were in San Fran on holiday. It only lasted about twenty minutes, but it was fun," Moore said.

"Yeah. Three hours in one of those things could give you a sore bum, that's for sure. We'll stop at a petrol station on the way to Baldonnel and get some sambos and stuff for the journey. We'll be about six hours in the air if all goes to plan – or at least I will be."

"Shit, Aidan, what is it that you're not telling me?"

"Oh, nothing. You'll see."

"Aw, c'mon. Don't be a prick. Spill the beans."

"OK. The revised plan. I take the two suspects back in the chopper."

"And…"

"And you go back on the ferry with the van."

"Hmm... doesn't sound too bad, I suppose."

"Are you OK driving a van?" Burke said.

"Yeah, I guess, how hard can it be?"

* * *

It was still dark when they arrived at Baldonnel. They could see that the helicopter was being readied for service. A fuel bowser was parked alongside with a wide hose leading into the body of the aircraft, and several men in green jumpsuits were milling around checking this and that.

Inside the building, Captain O'Donnell met them.

"Good morning, folks. A bit chilly, but not a bad day for it. We'll be ready for off at 07:00. Just a few things before we board. I'll need to take you through some brief safety and ditching instructions. We'll be hugging the coast nearly all the way, so I doubt there will be any problem. We'll probably have to re-fuel on the way back, but we can go into RAF Brawdy. They'll look after us. What's in the bag, Inspector?"

"Food. We brought some provisions."

"Well, that's fine, but we'll use our own. We can't take a chance on food from outside the camp, thanks all the same," O'Donnell said.

"Of course, sorry."

"No problem. Shall we get on board then and I'll take you through the safety procedures? As we're going over water, you'll need to put on these Crew Saver life harnesses. They inflate automatically if you end up in the drink."

"Great – that's comforting!" Moore said, looking askance at her boss.

* * *

With Burke and Moore safely strapped into the big machine, it lifted off at precisely seven o'clock. The chopper rose quickly into the early morning sky, and then banked steeply as it gathered speed and pointed its nose towards the coast. In the pre-dawn, the sky was starting to get streaked with yellow light out in the east.

The helicopter was more comfortable than either of the detectives had expected. They had pale green headsets on, so they could hear the two pilots talking to Dublin Air Traffic Control as they brought the machine up to its cruising height of 10,000 feet. The flight path took them down along the east coast of Ireland as far as Carnsore Point. From there they tracked the short distance across the Irish Sea to Strumble Head, and then turned south-east to fly along the southern coast of England.

This was the longest part of the journey, but it was interesting, because the seaside town of Weymouth was visible, and the co-pilot pointed it out as they passed noisily overhead. Soon after passing Weymouth, the big machine banked off to the south again and tracked directly towards Cherbourg, which protrudes well into the English Channel, due south of Bournemouth. As they crossed the Channel, they could make out the funnel of the ferry with its familiar logo, carrying their two suspects, steaming along towards their meeting point.

The helicopter flew in a large, low circle over the port, and descended steadily towards the helipad with the large white 'H' painted on it. As it neared the ground, a quantity of dust and wastepaper was blown into the air by the downwash from the rotors. O'Donnell landed the craft smoothly on the tarmac, and switched off the engines, providing a welcome silence after the long flight as the helicopter blades came slowly to a standstill.

When he had removed his headset, O'Donnell said to the passengers, "The wind is getting up quite strongly. The journey back will be a bit longer, and we'll definitely have to stop for fuel on the way. But we'll be fine. This old bird is steady enough in the wind. The ferry will be lively though!" he said, looking at Moore and smiling.

Moore looked out to sea, and as if to confirm the pilot's predictions, she could already see white horses forming on the waves, and when the door of the aircraft was opened, a strong breeze blew in.

The ferry was due in an hour and ten minutes, so the flight crew, the two soldiers and the Gardaí made their way into the terminal building. They got some coffee and croissants all round, and then a French police officer in a bright blue shirt with red epaulettes approached.

"You are the people from Dublin, yes?" he said with a strong French accent.

"Yes, that's right," Burke said.

"Very good. We have arranged for you to board the ferry when it docks before the doors are fully opened. You will find your targets sitting in their vehicle waiting to disembark. It would be good if you could be very discreet. We don't want a fuss here, if possible."

"Understood. We'll be as careful as we can. Thanks," Moore said.

"Good. I'll come back when it is docked, and I'll show you where to go. Enjoy your breakfast," the man said, and departed.

* * *

The long deep sound of the ferry's horn alerted them to the arrival of the ship. The water in the harbour was churned up creating white froth as the ferry manoeuvred onto the berth. As promised, the French policeman returned and escorted Burke and Moore to the side of the ship where a gangway of sorts had been placed against the ship's side, giving access directly to the car deck through a small pilot's door.

They found the van quickly, and slipped between the tightly packed vehicles, approaching it from behind. Burke tried the handle of the driver's door, and it opened easily.

Moore had gone around the other side of the Transit, and had gained access to Sinéad Walsh just as easily.

Burke wasted no time in handcuffing Freddy Taylor and manhandling him out of the van in the tight space between the vehicles. In a matter of just a few minutes, Taylor and Walsh had been escorted down the makeshift gangway and were secured inside the Air Corps helicopter. The flight crew started the engines and made ready for departure. Moore stood off and waved, as the machine rose into the air, banked away steeply and disappeared into the gathering clouds.

She went back up the rather shaky gangway, and climbed into the Transit. Soon, the visor door at the front of the vessel rose up slowly, the ramp dropped down, a claxon sounded and cars and vans began to leave the ship. When the deck was clear, Moore drove the van over to the side and reversed it into the slot allocated by the boarding crew, who had been told to arrange for it to travel back to Rosslare.

Moore locked up the van and climbed the steep interior stairs to the lounge area. She went and got herself a hot meal, and then found a seat beside a window with a reclining armchair, and settled down, intending to get some sleep. But the constant thud of the waves against the hull of the ship, and the at times wild lurching of the vessel as it was thrown around in the rough sea prevented her from nodding off. Later, as darkness fell, she managed a few short naps, but with the constant interruptions, and the sound of the wind whistling in the superstructure of the ferry, she hardly slept at all.

Chapter Twenty-Seven

The journey back from Cherbourg to Dublin in the helicopter was shorter, but no less unpleasant than the one Moore was enduring at sea. The wind was strong, and blowing from the south-west, so the big machine was constantly crabbing as it made its way back along the south coast of England.

To make matters worse, Sinéad Walsh had been thoroughly sick, and the stench of her vomit now pervaded the entire cabin of the aircraft. While this didn't seem to bother the flight crew, or the two soldiers from the Air Corps, it made Burke feel very nauseous, to the point where he thought he might throw up himself.

With Walsh indisposed, there was virtually no conversation between Burke and his travelling companions for the entire journey.

About halfway through the flight, the pilot came on the intercom and said that they would need to set down at RAF Brawdy in south Wales for fuel. Burke could hear the exchanges between the RAF control tower and O'Donnell over his headset. The pilot would have to bring the helicopter up to the north-east of the airfield so that he could land it into the wind and minimize the risk of being blown into the trees or the building as he approached the ground.

The approach was quite terrifying for Burke, Taylor and Walsh, all of whom had turned a sickly shade of green as O'Donnell wrestled with the controls to keep things on an even keel when descending towards the airstrip. They all breathed a joint sigh of relief when the machine finally touched down and came to rest.

While the helicopter was being refuelled, and the cabin cleaned up a bit, they all went indoors where the men from the RAF fussed over them, offering them all kinds of refreshments and making sure that they were as comfortable as possible.

Burke asked one of the young men if it was usually this rough when the wind was blowing hard from the south-west.

"It's usually much worse. You should see some of the weather we have to go up in to do rescues and the like. You wouldn't put a dog out. But the pilots are amazing, and the kit is well up to it. That's a very nice bird you're in today. We're still using those old Wessex jobs. More like a rattily old school bus than a modern helicopter."

Despite the man's reassurances, Burke wasn't looking forward to the last leg of the journey.

But when they got back on board after almost an hour, O'Donnell told them that the rest of the journey would be easier. The storm was passing away to the south, and he calculated that after about fifteen minutes in the air, they would be clear of it. To make things a bit better, he told them that he had adjusted the flight plan to travel up along the west coast of Wales as far as Anglesey, and then track directly from there to Baldonnel which he hoped to reach before darkness set in.

True to his word, the flight from St David's to Baldonnel was almost smooth, and the entire complement were feeling much better when they arrived back into Ireland, but there was still no chat between them.

Burke was met at Baldonnel by two Garda cars. Taylor and Walsh were separated with one of them in each car, and Burke took Moore's car back to Store Street. Mercifully, she had remembered to give him her keys before they left France.

* * *

After a most uncomfortable voyage back to Rosslare, the ferry finally found the shelter of the harbour, and Moore went below to take up her position on the car deck, in readiness for disembarkation.

She was exhausted, but the brightness, and the fresh air of the Wexford countryside cheered her up, and she decided to drive back to Dublin without trying to get a sleep in any of the many guest houses that were scattered around the port. The van drove well – it was much like a car, except that the visibility out the back was non-existent, so she had to get used to using the exterior mirrors more than she would normally. But it was comfortable, with a very good heater, and the radio pulled in every kind of station you could possibly want.

She was settling nicely into the trip as she approached the village of Ferns on the Wexford – Dublin road. Just as she approached the 50 kph speed limit sign, she noticed that the van started pulling to the left. As she progressed further towards the centre of the town, it got noticeably worse, until finally the cause of the problem dawned on her.

"Shit! That's all I need, a bloody puncture!"

Moore pulled the vehicle over to the side of the road where it was still quite wide, stopped the van and got out. True enough, the front nearside tyre was totally flat. Moore cursed her luck again. She had no intention of trying to change the wheel, so she went in search of the local Garda station. She didn't know the town, so she stopped an elderly woman with a shopping bag coming towards her, and said, "Excuse me, can you tell me where the Garda station is, please?"

"Isn't it down at the bottom of the hill by the bridge, where it's always been?" the woman said, as if everyone should know that.

"Thank you," Moore said, managing to suppress a smirk.

She introduced herself to the fresh-faced young Garda sitting at the desk reading a copy of the Wexford People. Moore explained her plight to the young man.

"That's no bother. Me and Jim will go and change the wheel for you. Can you stay here and man the desk – there'll be nothing happening anyway. Where did you say it was?"

"Just up on the Wexford Road near the speed limit sign. It's a white Transit with 'Sprinter Transport' signwriting."

The young Garda collected his colleague from the back of the station. Moore handed over the keys. The two men put on their jackets and left.

It was less than half an hour later when the two returned to the Garda station. There had been no activity at all while they were gone, so Moore made herself a mug of coffee in the makeshift kitchen, and sat back and relaxed.

The young Garda who she had met initially had a broad grin on his face, and was holding a black plastic refuse sack in his hand.

"That was a good one, all right," he said to Moore.

Moore looked at him with a puzzled expression.

"There was no spare wheel in the cubby behind the driver's seat, but we did find this," he said, holding up the bag.

"What's in it?" Moore said.

"Have a look."

The Garda opened the neck of the bag, and Moore leaned forward to peer in.

"Jesus! There must be over a hundred grand there. And it was just where the spare should have been, right?"

"Yep."

"OK, thanks, well, don't handle it too much, I'll need to take it back with me for evidence. And what are we going to do about the puncture? I take it the spare wheel wasn't anywhere to be found."

"Don't worry about that, Sergeant. I'll get one of the lads from the garage to pop down and take the wheel off. He can take it back to the workshop and fix the puncture for you. It won't take long."

"And how much will that cost?" Moore said, conscious that she had a limited amount of cash on her, except for the contents of the bag.

"Don't give it a thought. They'll be happy to oblige. They owe us a few favours, and if necessary we can get them to add it on to the next servicing bill for the squad car. But I doubt it will come to that."

Moore had forgotten how things worked between the Gardaí and the locals once you got well clear of Dublin. She could imagine the symbiotic relationship that existed between the Gardaí and the local mechanics, and couldn't help but be slightly envious. In Dublin, any approach from the Gardaí to the car repair shops was usually met with a profanity.

"That would be great, thanks very much."

The young Garda went off to make the arrangements, and in no time at all, a small, wiry youth in a pair of very dirty red overalls appeared in the door carrying the keys of the van in his grimy hand.

"All done, Liam. She's right for the road. It was a nail as thick as your finger stuck in it," the mechanic said, holding out his index finger to make the point. "But it's grand now, and I brought it down for you too. It's just outside."

"Thanks very much, Mark, you're a star."

"Ah, no bother. See ya later."

Moore thanked the young Garda profusely for his assistance and prepared to leave.

"Would you like one of us to go with you, Sergeant, in case it breaks down again? Young Jim here could go, and then get the train back later," Liam said.

"No, you're grand. I'll lock the doors and I'll be back in the city in no time."

Chapter Twenty-Eight

Burke was very much aware that he couldn't hold Taylor and Walsh for much longer without getting an extension from the Super. When he had received the call from Moore informing him about the bag of money that had been found in the van, it gave him just cause, and he decided to ask Heffernan for another twenty-four hours. He wanted Moore with him when the real questioning took place. Despite his often-dismissive attitude towards his sergeant, he valued her input greatly, and he felt she would appreciate the gesture given the rough journey she had had back with the van.

Moore arrived back into Store Street just after five o'clock. She brought the bag of money inside with her and went looking for Burke.

"Hi. I brought you a present," she said when she found him in the canteen.

"So I hear. You'd better get that counted, and then bring it over to forensics. Let's see whose prints are on it, and if possible, where it came from. Get Dónal to count it with you. That way you won't be able to pocket a few hundred for your holiday fund," Burke said.

"Ha ha. Very funny. How are the two runaways?"

"Brooding. They are lawyered up now, and have said very little. But they don't know we found their stash. I'd like to go in hot and heavy tomorrow morning with you. OK?"

"Sure, no problem."

"Did you have any more trouble with the van?"

"No, it was grand. Those guys in Ferns were really helpful. Very chivalrous – unlike some I could name!"

"Well, if I was manning a station where the worst that ever happened was a missing dog, or a broken traffic light, I could be prince charming too. Now, off with ye. See you bright and early tomorrow," Burke said cheerfully.

She didn't quite see Burke as prince charming under any circumstances. She went to get Dónal to do the count with her before sending the cash over to forensics.

Then she went home for a long, well-earned sleep.

* * *

Sylvester McNabb was not a solicitor to be trifled with. He had arrived before nine o'clock, demanding a parking place for his shiny Mercedes S-Class in the station car park. He was a tall man, immaculately dressed in an expensive grey three-piece suit with a smart white shirt and silk tie, and very shiny black leather shoes. Just by the way he carried himself, the detectives knew he would be troublesome, and they weren't wrong.

McNabb asked for half an hour to confer with his clients before the police started to question them. He established that Taylor would be first up, and requested refreshments for both Taylor and himself, which Moore was sent to arrange.

Burke and Moore brought takeaway coffees into the interview room, more to establish their equality with the surly solicitor than to quench their thirst.

"Inspector, you have arrested my client illegally in a foreign country without a European arrest warrant, so I must insist that you release him immediately. This is outrageous, I've never heard the like of it," McNabb said.

"Mr McNabb, your client was arrested on an Irish vessel before he had a chance to abscond, along with his partner in crime. It was perfectly legitimate, and even if there is some doubt, and we were to release him as you are demanding, I can assure you he would be re-arrested before he had descended the steps of this Garda station. Now we can go through all that nonsense if you insist, but I'd rather not play silly games," Burke said.

"You haven't heard the end of this, Inspector Burke, rest assured."

The two men were going at each other like rutting stags, so Moore decided she had better step in.

"Mr Taylor, how many employees did McCranny Construction have that were billeted in the old warehouse down by the river?"

"How should I know?"

"Well, for starters, according to a statement we have from one of those men, you turned up every week at the place and paid them for their week's work in cash – if you could call it pay," Moore said.

"No comment," Taylor replied.

"And can you tell us what nationalities McCranny's workforce is made up of, Mr Taylor?"

Taylor just shrugged his shoulders and looked down at the floor.

"Where were you going when we found you on the ferry, Mr Taylor?" Moore said.

"France."

"Obviously, but where after that?"

"Nowhere special."

Burke had had enough.

"Look, Mr Taylor, as you well know, we found over a hundred thousand euro concealed in the van you were driving. Now I'd appreciate if you would stop obstructing our enquiries, and tell us what you know," Burke said.

McNabb intervened.

"Did you actually find my client in possession of the money?"

"No, but it was in the van that he had been driving."

"My client denies any knowledge of any money in the van. It's not his and he doesn't know how it might have got there."

"What? You think that people just go leaving that kind of money lying around on the floor of a Transit van for anyone to find?" Burke said.

"It wasn't on the flo–" Taylor said.

McNabb buried his face in his hands, but recovered quickly.

"No, it wasn't, was it. It was behind the driver's seat, and by now our forensic people will have identified your fingerprints all over the plastic wrappers and on the bag, so you may as well admit it, Mr Taylor," Moore said.

McNabb responded on Taylor's behalf, "There's nothing wrong with taking money away when you're travelling, it's perfectly normal."

"Not in that quantity it isn't – and not in cash. Did McCranny know he was employing illegals? Maybe he found out, and didn't agree with it, so you had to silence him. Is that what happened, Mr Taylor?" Burke said.

"Inspector, I presume you have some proof that McCranny Construction was employing illegal immigrants. I understood that all of their work was carried out by sub-contractors, and Mr McCranny can hardly be responsible for whatever they get up to, now can he?" McNabb said.

"So why was your client paying them, in that case?" Moore said.

"My client denies any such thing. If he did give them money, it was purely altruistic. He was simply helping some men who had fallen on hard times by giving them a temporary hand out, that's all."

"Interview suspended at 9:52 a.m. Come on, Sergeant, I've had enough of this crap," Burke said.

"Are you charging my client, Inspector?" McNabb said.
"All in good time, Mr McNabb, all in good time."

* * *

"This isn't going well, Fiona. We need some kind of breakthrough, and I can't see McNabb letting anything slip. Any ideas?" Burke said when they were back in his office.

"Why don't I have a go at Walsh on my own? I know McNabb will sit in, but I think I might be able to get into her head. It's worth a try, anyway. What do you say?" Moore said.

"Good luck with that. But you're right, it's worth a try, I suppose."

Moore went back downstairs and collected McNabb who was still in conference with Freddy Taylor.

"I need to question Miss Walsh now. I presume you want to be in attendance, Mr McNabb?"

"Certainly. Where is she?"

"Next door. Come on, I'll show you."

Sinéad Walsh was not in very robust condition when Moore went into the interview room with the solicitor. The solicitor took up the usual position sitting close to his client, while Moore sat facing the two of them.

"Miss Walsh, I need to ask you some questions about operations at McCranny Construction. Were you aware that Gerald McCranny was employing illegal immigrants to work on the building sites?"

"My client has no comment," McNabb said.

"Wait, Mr McNabb. It's all right. Yes, I knew about it," the girl said, looking down at the table.

"I see. And what exactly was your involvement in it?"

"Really, Miss Walsh, I would advise you to say no more, no more at all," the solicitor said, looking more animated than he had all morning.

"I did the payroll for them. And I helped to arrange some of the travel to get them into the country. But

Freddy was the brains behind it. After the financial crash of 2008, McCranny's almost went bust. We had several contracts that needed finishing, and we hadn't the money to pay for the work at Irish rates. Freddy had this idea to import labour from Eastern Europe. He made some contacts, and before we knew where we were, there were van loads of Romanians and Turks arriving to work for us."

"I see. So, you say Mr Taylor was behind all of this?"

"Yes. Yes, he was. I did the payroll and kept the books. But I didn't have anything to do with the immigrants."

"What exactly is your relationship with Mr Taylor, Sinéad?"

McNabb wasted no time in attempting to cut off that line of questioning.

"Really, Sergeant, what possible relevance can that have to your enquiries. I must protest."

"It's OK. We can't keep it a secret for ever. We were lovers," the girl said in a very matter-of-fact way.

"I see. And did Mr McCranny know about this?"

"Search me. Maybe, I don't know, but we tried to be discreet."

"I presume Freddy Taylor is married?" Moore said.

"Yes, he is. So what? He wouldn't be the first married man to play away, now would he?" Sinéad said.

"Maybe McCranny found out and was threatening to tell Mrs Taylor. Is that it?"

At this, McNabb became quite agitated. Things weren't going well for his client.

"Sergeant, that's pure speculation, and you know it. Now I urge you to discontinue this line of questioning and move on," he said.

"Hit a nerve, have I, Mr McNabb?" Moore said, and then turning back to Sinéad Walsh, "So is that what happened, Sinéad? McCranny was going to tell Mrs Taylor about your affair, so you had to shut him up?"

"No, no, I've told you – we had nothing to do with his death."

Moore decided that she needed to change tack. But she wasn't finished with this line of questioning.

"Where were the two of you planning to go when we intercepted you?" Moore said.

"Don't you mean illegally arrested my clients on foreign soil, Sergeant?" McNabb said, unable to resist the jibe.

Moore ignored the man.

"Well?"

"We were going to drive south, to the Loire Valley. Freddy has a small cottage there near Blois. He showed me photographs. It's quite a humble place in a quiet spot out in the country, but typically French. We were going to lie low for a while till all this blew over, and then start again. He's a very good architect."

"How did you manage to get hold of the money we found in the van?"

"Simple, really. We cooked the books. When the building trade improved, McCranny wanted to pay the men properly for their work. So, I drew cash as if they were getting regular wages, but Freddy only paid them a couple of hundred a week. We syphoned off the rest. I know it was wrong, but it was so easy, and the men were happy with what they were getting."

"What happened then? Did McCranny find out? Is that why you had to kill him?" Moore said.

"I strongly advise you to say nothing, Miss Walsh, for your own sake," McNabb interjected.

"No, no. We had nothing to do with that. Absolutely nothing."

"Well, how do you explain the fact that Mr McCranny was poisoned then? Someone must have done it."

"Of course, but it had nothing to do with Freddy or me, I swear."

Moore was inclined to believe the girl, so she decided to change her approach for the second time.

"Tell me about Mr McCranny, Sinéad," Moore said.

"What do you want to know?"

"What was he like to work for?"

"Good. He was good, most of the time. He sometimes got a bit tense when things were going badly, especially when his daughter came around, but I suppose everyone does, don't they?" Walsh said.

"His daughter – did she call to the office?"

"Yes, occasionally. She used to come in to use the office equipment for her college work – you know, the photocopier, the binding machine, that sort of thing."

"Did they argue?"

"No, not specially. But Mr McCranny always seemed to be a bit on edge when she was there. Not as relaxed as normal. I just put it down to family friction."

"When did she last visit the office?"

"I don't know for sure. She had her own set of keys, you see, in case she needed to get in on the weekends to finish an assignment or something."

"And you have no idea who might have disliked Gerald McCann enough to murder him?"

"No, of course not. The whole thing seems surreal to me. I can't believe what's happened," Sinéad said.

"OK. Well, let's leave it at that for now. We have some further enquiries to make, and the Immigration Department may need to speak to you," Moore said.

"What will happen to me?" Walsh said. She was becoming tearful as she contemplated her fate.

"That remains to be seen. There will be charges, naturally, but your cooperation will be taken into account."

Chapter Twenty-Nine

"How did you get on?" Burke asked Moore.

"Interesting. I think she'll put Taylor right in the frame if she thinks she can get away with it, but my guess is she was up to her neck in it. Hard to prove, though. She mentioned that McCranny's daughter used to visit the office. I think we should talk to her."

"What could she have to do with anything?" Burke said.

"I dunno. But it's a loose end. I'd like to follow it up."

"Suit yourself. I'd better get Ann Quinlan over to interview those two before our time runs out. We can catch up later."

"Right. See you."

* * *

"Mrs McCranny, it's Sergeant Moore here from Store Street. By any chance, is your daughter there with you?"

"Emily? She's had to go into college. Despite everything, she has exams coming up, and she's very anxious about them. She'll be studying."

"Oh, OK. Could you give me her mobile phone number please, Mrs McCranny?"

"Yes, of course. Just hold on a sec."

Moore waited while the woman rummaged around in her handbag for her phone.

"Here it is. 0-8-8-7-5-2-8-1-2-2. Got it?"

"Yes, thanks. Remind me again what it is she is actually studying."

"Bio-science. Don't ask me what that's all about. She's a clever girl, but she didn't get her brains from me. Is there anything else, Sergeant?"

"No, that's all, Mrs McCranny. Sorry to have disturbed you. Bye."

Moore dialled Emily McCranny's number. After five rings, it went through to voicemail.

"Hi, this is Emily. I can't come to the phone just now. You know what to do. Bye-ee," the voice said.

"Hi, Emily. This is Sergeant Moore from Store Street Garda station. I wonder if you could give me a call on my mobile when you get this. Thanks." Moore recited her own mobile number and then terminated the call.

Moore was getting up to go and get herself a coffee when Ann Quinlan came into the office.

"Hello, Fiona. I hear you lifted Freddy Taylor and Sinéad Walsh off the ferry in France."

"Yes, that's right, ma'am. We've been interviewing them. Taylor hasn't said much, but the girl is more talkative. She reckons it was all Taylor's idea, and I think she has more to tell."

"OK. Well, firstly, please don't call me ma'am, it makes me sound ancient. Ann will do nicely. Is Inspector Burke in his office? I think he wants to hand them over to us."

"Yes, I think so, but I'm a bit surprised at that," Moore said.

"Why so?" Quinlan said.

"Well, we still may need them in connection with the murder of Gerald McCranny. It's not at all certain they weren't involved."

"Don't worry. They aren't going to disappear. But we need to act fast if we are to use their evidence to close down their routes. You'd be amazed how quickly these gangs can change their arrangements," Quinlan said.

"Oh, I see. And what about Demir," Moore said.

"Demir. Oh, him. What about him?"

"Did Inspector Burke not talk to you about him – Bilal Demir? He's the one who identified Taylor for us. The inspector told me that he promised Demir that he will try and get his family over here and get them refugee status. That's why the man was so helpful," Moore said.

"Yes, I was with him when he said that. I told him he had no right to make those kinds of promises. I'd better go and have a word."

* * *

Quinlan went off to find Burke. Moore hoped she hadn't dropped him right in it with Immigration, but she had felt uneasy about his discussions with Bilal Demir from the start.

Moore's phone rang.

"Hello, is this Sergeant Moore?" the caller said.

"Yes, who's calling please?"

"This is Emily McCranny. You were looking for me."

"Yes, Emily. Thanks for calling back. I wonder if we could meet?" Moore said.

"Well, yes, I suppose so. I'm very busy revising for my Christmas exams, though. Will it take long?"

"No, not at all, and I can come to you. Minimise your downtime."

"OK. Do you know the Buttery here in college?"

"Yes, I think so. It's just down the steps off Front Square, isn't it?" Moore said.

"Yes, that's right. I could meet you there at, say, 2:30. By then the lunchtime crowd will have finished and it will be quieter," Emily said.

"Fine. 2:30 it is then."

"How will you know me?"

"Don't worry. We can use our phones to sort that out. See you later."

* * *

Quinlan found Aidan Burke in his office.

"Hi, Aidan. I hear you have two people traffickers for me. Nice one," she said.

"Hi, Ann. Well, not so fast. The main man hasn't actually admitted anything yet, but I reckon a few more rounds of questioning should shake him loose."

"Look, Aidan, I'd like to take this over now if you don't mind. We need to act immediately if we're going to catch the people behind the trafficking," Quinlan said.

"Hmm. I hear you. But these two turkeys may be involved in the murder of Gerald McCranny. McCranny was poisoned. Arsenic injected into his cigars, which were kept at the office where both of these two had easy access to them. I haven't even started on that with them yet."

"OK. So, what's your plan?"

"I'm going to rattle them stupid about the immigrants. Then when they are feeling all shaky and vulnerable, go in for the kill about McCranny. I bet I get a confession before nightfall."

Quinlan stayed quiet, processing what Burke had said, and planning her next move.

"Tell you what. Why don't you let me do the softening up? Or we could do it together. Then I'll leave you to pounce when I have what I need. Deal?"

"OK. Let's see how it goes. We'll tackle Taylor first. He'll be harder to crack, but he's also the one with all the info I need. You ready?" Burke said.

"Yep, let's go."

Chapter Thirty

Trinity College Dublin is by far the oldest university in Ireland. Established by Queen Elizabeth of England in 1592, and modelled along the same lines as Oxford and Cambridge, the single college of Trinity is still connected to St John's College, Cambridge and Oriel College, Oxford.

Some of the oldest buildings on the city centre campus are positioned around Front Square – a large, cobbled, open area standing inside the main gate which opens off College Green. Moore had a vague knowledge of the place, and remembered that The Buttery – a substantial basement level restaurant that catered for academics and students alike – was to the left off Front Square as you entered the College with the front gate behind you.

It was a fine, clear afternoon in Dublin. Moore walked across from Store Street to keep her rendezvous with the young student. When she entered the campus, Moore was struck by the relative tranquillity of the place after the cacophony of the traffic outside the perimeter. The sun was shining on the magnificent old buildings, and students, many of them texting busily on their phones, were hurrying to lectures, carrying books, criss-crossing the square.

Moore descended the granite steps into the restaurant. She didn't have to resort to her phone to find Emily. A solitary student was sitting at a table nursing a half-finished cup of black coffee, looking anxiously about her.

"Emily?" Moore said.

"Yes, Sergeant Moore. How did you recognise me?" the girl said.

"Well, I am a detective," Moore said with a smile. She pulled out one of the spare chairs and sat down.

Emily McCranny was a good-looking girl. She had long, shiny chestnut-coloured hair, and an oval face with high cheekbones; big brown eyes, and a full mouth. She was dressed more expensively than many of her peers in the college, with well-cut blue denim jeans and what looked to Moore like a Giorgio Armani top.

"Thanks for seeing me, Emily. I'm very sorry about your father, I'm sure you miss him terribly." As she said this, Moore studied the girl carefully to see what kind of reaction there was, but could perceive virtually nothing.

"When did you last see your dad?" Moore said.

"Some time ago. We hadn't really been getting on lately, not since… well, you know?"

"Since what, Emily?"

"You must already know that my father had taken to relationships with young men, Sergeant. Not exactly what a girl would hope for in her parent, is it?" Emily's eyes flared when she said this. It was clear she was angry about the situation.

"And you didn't approve?"

"No, I bloody didn't. Would you?"

"I'm not sure how I would react, to be honest. My father died when I was a child. I never really got to know him very well at all. But I might have been able to accept it, I don't know."

"Well, I didn't, that's for sure. It disgusts me. It's horrible. I feel tainted."

Moore sensed that the girl was getting quite het up, so she tried to get the conversation back on the original track.

"So, when exactly did you see him last?"

"Months ago. It was Mum's birthday. We had a family dinner. But at that time, I wasn't sure about his sexuality. Nothing had been said."

"When were your suspicions confirmed?"

"One night at the end of the summer. I had an assignment to hand in, so I went to his offices to print it off – it was nearly fifty pages. I sometimes go there to use the office equipment. I like my assignments to look professional," Emily said.

"What time of the day was this?"

"It was late – around half past eight, I think. I have my own set of keys, and I have the alarm code too, so I can let myself in at any time."

"What happened?"

"When I got inside, I noticed that there was a light on in Dad's office, and I could hear peculiar noises coming from the room. I thought maybe he was having a bad turn or something, so I opened the door and found them at it." Emily's cheeks flushed, and her eyes filled with tears at the memory of what she had seen that night.

"At what exactly?"

"Use your imagination, Sergeant. Having sex. He was with some ghastly scruffy young type, and my dad was on top of him on the floor. It was horrific." Emily retrieved a tissue from her pockets and sniffed into it.

"Did he know you were there?"

"No, I don't think so. I didn't know whether to call out to him or what. But I didn't. I just left the office and went home. But I was very shaken. It wasn't a nice spectacle."

"No, I suppose not. And had you seen him since that night at all?"

"Not likely. I mean he came and went at home, and we bumped into each other. But I hadn't spoken to him since that night, and do you know something, Sergeant?"

"What's that."

"I'm glad he's dead!" And with that the girl put her head forward onto the top of the table and heartfelt sobs wracked her body.

Moore pulled her chair around so she could comfort the girl. She put her arm around her shoulder, and just held her until the sobbing subsided. Emily wiped her tear-filled eyes, and slowly sat up.

"I'm sorry," she whimpered. "I'll be fine now, sorry."

"No, don't apologise. Are you OK?"

"Yes. Was there anything else?"

"Well, maybe. Do you know of anyone who might have wanted to harm your father? Did he have any enemies that you are aware of?" Moore said.

"God, I have no idea. I don't know any of his business associates, except for Sinéad and Melissa, and of course Freddy Taylor."

"Right. OK, then, I think we're done. Look, I'm sorry if I upset you. Are you sure you're OK? Would you like me to get you a drink of water or something?"

"No, thanks. I'm OK, really," Emily said.

Moore fetched a business card from her pocket, and gave it to the girl.

"If you remember anything, no matter how insignificant it may seem, please give me a call, anytime day or night," Moore said.

"OK. Thanks."

Moore walked back through the cool afternoon sunshine. As she walked along she processed the discussion that had taken place with the girl. She could find nothing amiss with what Emily had said, but for some reason which Moore couldn't put her finger on, she had an uneasy feeling about it.

* * *

Back in the open plan, Teresa, the civilian worker attached to the unit, approached Moore.

"Hi, Sarge. Got a second?"

"Yes, sure. What's up?" Moore said.

"Well, you know you asked me to have a trawl through the phone records from McCranny's office. I did find something a bit strange, at least I think it looked odd," the girl said.

"Oh. What was that?"

"About a week before McCranny was killed. There are a couple of calls to a mobile number made from the office phone at eleven o'clock at night."

"Are you sure of the time?"

"Fairly certain. The information comes from the phone company, and all the other timings look correct."

"And is it the same mobile number?"

"Yes. The first call lasted twenty-two seconds, but the second one was much longer – just over eight minutes," Teresa said.

"Interesting. Do we have any information on the mobile number – as in who it belongs to?"

"No, but I might be able to find out."

"Yes, do that. Get help from the techies if you need it. Oh and, Teresa, see if there's any chance that the alarm system at the offices records the times that the system was set and de-activated as well. That might tell us what time our mystery caller entered the building."

"Right, Sarge. I'll get back to you."

Chapter Thirty-One

Sylvester McNabb, Freddy Taylor, Anne Quinlan and Aidan Burke were all crowded into the small interview room in the basement of Store Street Garda station. Introductions had been made, and McNabb became quite uneasy when he learnt of Ann Quinlan's role in the matter. McNabb had asked for refreshments for his client, but Burke surmised that it was the solicitor who was more in need of coffee to reinvigorate him. Things hadn't been going well, and he wasn't used to not having things his own way.

McNabb started with the same old tactic, accusing Burke of falsely arresting his client without the proper paperwork, and demanding that Taylor be released immediately. Burke decided that he had quite enough of the suave lawyer, and had noticed his discomfort on meeting Ann Quinlan.

"Have you represented many people traffickers recently, Mr McNabb?" Burke asked, much to the surprise of his colleague from Immigration.

"My client denies vehemently having any involvement with any such business, Inspector. It's preposterous!"

"That would be a 'no' then, Mr McNabb," Burke went on, keen to wrong-foot the man.

"As I have said, Inspector, your wild and totally unsubstantiated allegations are plainly ridiculous. And my client list is none of your business."

"Oh, but it is, Mr McNabb. You see, Freddy, what I think you have here is a corporate lawyer. He's probably very good at preparing contracts, or doing a bit of property conveyancing, but I doubt if he has any idea about the squalor, the rape and torture of innocent men, women and children, the exploitation, the starvation, the humiliation, the casual approach to the death of migrants with which you have become involved. Have you, Mr McNabb?"

"This is outrageous! You have no evidence whatsoever that my client is involved in any of this. I'll be making a complaint to your superiors about your conduct, Inspector Burke."

Burke turned coolly to Ann Quinlan, "Be sure to remind me to give Mr McNabb a complaint form on his way out, won't you, Ann?"

"Now, as to your client's involvement in people trafficking, Mr McNabb, we have several witness statements, we have documentary evidence, we have the testimony from Miss Walsh – Taylor's partner in crime, and of course we have in excess of €100,000 in cash that was found in Taylor's possession when we arrested him on Irish soil perfectly legally the day before yesterday," Burke said.

Then he leaned in close to McNabb and looked him directly in the eye.

"But I don't give a flying fuck about any of that. That's my colleague, Inspector Quinlan's department, and you should know she's very good at her job, Mr McNabb. What I'm interested in, is who killed Gerald McCranny. And right now, your client looks just about right for it to me. So, if you don't mind awfully, I'll get on with interrogating him before my tea goes cold."

Taylor looked pleadingly at the solicitor, who appeared to have more or less given up following Burke's little speech.

"Right, Mr Taylor, I want you to tell me everything – and I mean everything – about your relationship with McCranny Construction Limited, and the other companies run by Mr McCranny, and then I want you to tell me about your personal relationship with Mr McCranny, and anything else you think may be relevant."

Freddy Taylor started into a long and meandering tale about how he had first met Gerald McCranny just as the property boom was getting really fired up in Dublin in 2005. They had worked together on many projects, with Taylor being the lead architect on nearly all of McCranny's buildings.

After twenty minutes of these reminiscences, McNabb cut in again.

"Is all this really necessary, Inspector? Can you not just ask your questions so we can get out of here sometime today?"

"Just giving your client every opportunity to explain himself, Mr McNabb. But if you're in a hurry to leave, don't let us keep you."

The solicitor sat back in his chair grumpily.

"Carry on, Mr Taylor, but perhaps you could skip to the present day, and tell us how you came to fall out with Mr McCranny."

"I didn't. We had the occasional disagreement, but we never fell out. That's just not true."

"Really? Then maybe you could enlighten us about who might have hated him enough to kill him?"

"I've no idea," Taylor said.

"Right. Well, I'm away to prepare some charges related to the fraud. I'm sure Inspector Quinlan can keep you occupied for a little while longer while I'm gone. We'll be applying to have you remanded, by the way. You are an obvious flight risk, so we won't have any trouble there.

You'd better get used to the inside of a cell, Mr Taylor. It's a far cry from an architect's office, I can assure you."

Then Burke got up and left the room, leaving Inspector Ann Quinlan to pursue her enquiries.

* * *

"Well, did you get a confession to murder?" Moore asked when they met up again back in Burke's office.

"No, I bloody didn't. But I did nearly murder that smarmy lawyer of his. Prick!"

"Yes, he's a right little charmer, isn't he?"

"What have you got?" Burke asked.

"I went and had a chat with McCranny's daughter. She really didn't enjoy finding out her father was gay." Moore went on to describe how the girl had discovered the truth about her dad.

"Blimey. A bit of a shocker for sure. Anything else?"

"Nothing useful. But Teresa may be on to something. She's found a record of calls being made from McCranny's office late at night a few days before he was bumped off."

"Probably nothing. I'd put my money on those two downstairs if only we could find a way in. Ann is having a go at Taylor now. What about Walsh?"

"She'll tell us all we need to know to try and save her own ass. She says it was all Freddy's idea, and she'll cough up lots of evidence to try and frame him. They were an item too, by the way, and of course Taylor is married."

"Lovely. Well, she can't escape the ferry business, and the cash. I'd better go upstairs and put Heffernan in the picture – he won't be best pleased."

"Good luck with that. See you later then."

* * *

"Damn it, Aidan, you have enough criminality there for several charges, and you still can't find who killed the man. What are you at?" Heffernan said when Burke sat down opposite him in his spacious office.

"I know, sir, it's not going too well. But at least we got someone for the young lad."

"Ah, don't be talking. The old guy will probably get three or four years at most, and a decent lawyer will get him off on temporary insanity – I've seen that too many times before – wait till you see."

"And there's more bad news, I'm afraid, sir. McNabb, Taylor's lawyer, is going to put in a complaint about how we arrested his clients, and he has a point."

"Don't worry about that. We get on very well with the French police. I'll get them to issue some sort of paperwork that'll tie yer man up in knots for years if he tries anything. He'll not catch us out that handy," Heffernan said.

"That would be very helpful, sir. It wouldn't be good if it got as far as Merrion Square – an 'International Incident' and all that shite."

"You're right – but it won't. I'll close it down, but I need something from you in return, Aidan."

"What's that, sir?"

"Well. Two things, actually. Firstly, I want you to make Ann Quinlan look good. She's going for a big promotion in Immigration, and the brass want her to get it – gender balance, and all that – so a good result here would pretty well guarantee it."

"OK. Well, that won't be hard. She had them pretty well banged to rights, and with blondie singing like a canary, it's game over for Taylor in any case. What's the other thing, sir?"

"Get this McCranny thing sorted out, will ye? I need it fixed up soon. I won't go into the details, but it's important."

"Right, I hear you. Now, can I ask you to do something for me too?" Burke said.

"Jesus, Burke, are you sure you're not from Cork?"

"It's just this guy Bilal Demir. He's been very helpful to us. In fact, without him, we wouldn't have got on to

Taylor, and he would probably right now be sitting in his cottage in France sipping a nice glass of red wine and counting his hundred grand. It would be terrific if we could get Demir some papers. Then his wife could come across and join him. He's a decent bloke."

"Hmm. Well, off you go and see to my two requests, and if all goes well, I'll probably be able to square off the other business for you. What did you say his name was?"

"Demir – D-E-M-I-R, Bilal. He's Turkish, I think!"

Heffernan wrote the name down in his day book, and as he did so, Burke realised that it would be taken care of. Heffernan never noted anything that wasn't going to be sorted.

Chapter Thirty-Two

Teresa came across to where Moore was sitting at her desk in the open plan.

"Darren. Darren Richardson," she said.

"What about him?" Moore replied.

"That's who the phone calls were made to from McCranny's office late at night."

"Oh, right. Thanks – well done. Do we have an address?"

"Yes – but it's in Sligo, I'm afraid," Teresa said.

"Shit! But hold on, I have a hunch. Get onto Trinity College and see if they have a Darren Richardson on their books. And if that draws a blank, check out UCD and DCU as well."

"Do you think he's a student then?" Teresa said.

"Maybe. We'll see."

Teresa was back a few minutes later.

"Bingo! You were right. Richardson is a student at Trinity, and he has rooms in Trinity Hall up in Dartry."

"Excellent. I need the room number or whatever, and then I think we'll go and pay Mr Richardson a visit. You didn't by any chance discover what he's studying in college, did you?"

"No, sorry boss, should I have?"

"No. Don't worry, it's fine. Just get me his room number. Thanks."

* * *

Trinity Hall is comprised of a number of low-rise apartment blocks situated close to the River Dodder in the suburb of Dartry. It's an idyllic location, and although it's nowhere near the university campus, it provides good quality accommodation for those students who can afford it.

Moore asked Burke if he wanted to come with her when she went to find out a bit more about the student, but he declined, saying that he had some things to do for the Super.

It took Moore about twenty minutes to drive out to Dartry. She swung her car in through the gates, and was pleased to find that the units were all logically numbered. She had no difficulty finding Richardson's apartment, but unfortunately, there was no one at home.

Undeterred, she called his mobile number, and after two rings, the phone was answered by a well-spoken young man who recited his name.

"Darren, this is Detective Sergeant Moore from Store Street Garda. Can I ask where you are just now?"

"Yes, of course. I'm in Dartry, Trinity Hall."

"OK, but there's no reply at your apartment."

"No. I'm with a mate at his. How can I help?"

"Could you come back to your own place? We need to have a little chat."

"Sounds ominous. Yes, sure. I'll be there in a few minutes."

While Moore was waiting for Darren to arrive, she looked around the complex. It was well for students these days, she thought. When she had been going through college, she had had to share a grotty flat in Ranelagh with four other extremely slovenly girls from the country who had never been away from home before in their lives. The place was constantly filthy, and the comings and goings were disgraceful, although Moore managed to retain her own rather straight-laced standards, and avoid much of the debauchery.

Darren Richardson arrived to interrupt Moore's musings. He was very tall – probably around six foot two – slim and handsome, although he had a somewhat scruffy appearance. As he approached, he extinguished a rolled-up cigarette, and exhaled the smoke away from Moore's face. Then turning towards her, he extended his outstretched hand, "Hi. I'm Darren Richardson. You must be Detective Moore."

The door opened into quite a spacious apartment that was remarkably tidy and even clean, given the nature of its occupants.

Richardson gestured to a comfy chair, and said, "Take a seat. Can I get you a coffee or maybe a beer, Detective?"

Moore was struck by the confidence the lad exuded. He was definitely meeting her on equal terms.

"No, thanks. I'm fine. I just need to ask you a few questions."

Richardson sat at one of the breakfast bar stools, so that he was noticeably higher up than Moore. She wondered if it was deliberate.

"How can I help?" he said again, opening his arms and spreading his hands.

"Darren, do you know a Gerald McCranny?"

"No. I know Emily pretty well though. We're going out together. I think her father's name is Gerald, but I've never met him."

"I see. How long have you been going with Emily?"

"Since last year. We met at a party."

"Have you ever been to her father's offices?"

"No, I told you, I've never met him."

"So, you've never gone in with Emily after hours for anything?"

"No. Why would I do that?"

"Maybe to use some of the office equipment for college stuff, that sort of thing."

"No. I wouldn't need to. I get all that stuff done in Read's on Nassau Street, outside College."

"Are you aware that Emily goes into her dad's place sometimes after hours, Darren?"

"I think she might have said something about that. I'm not sure to be honest."

"OK. Can I ask you to cast your mind back a few weeks? You got a call – well, two actually – from Emily at about 11 p.m. She was calling from her father's premises on that occasion. Do you remember?"

"Hang on. Yes, I do. When the first call came through, I didn't recognize the number, so I didn't answer it. But when I got the second call, I thought I'd better if only to stop whoever it was calling."

"Do you remember what the call was about?"

"Not really. I think Em was just feeling a bit down. She wasn't confident about one of her exams and got a bit depressed about it."

"Did you meet up after the call?"

"No. No we didn't."

"I see. Do you mind me asking what you are studying in college?"

"Chemical Sciences. I'm hoping to specialize in Biology or Bioscience for my final year."

"Have you ever worked with arsenic, Darren?"

"That's a funny question, but no, I haven't. I think I've seen it in the lab, but I don't use it for anything. Why do you ask?"

"Just following enquiries, Darren. Is there anything else you can tell me about Emily's relationship with her father?"

"Nothing, I'm afraid. I know they weren't close, that's about it."

"Any idea why that was?"

"No, none. She never said."

"OK. Well, that's all I can think of for now, Darren. Thanks for agreeing to see me. If I need anything further, I'll be back in touch."

Moore got up from her seat, and made for the door. Richardson followed behind her, and as she opened the door, she turned around and shook hands with him.

"Nice accommodation you have here. You must enjoy it."

"Yes, it's great. Better than being in some grim flat in Rathmines, that's for sure."

A shiver went down Moore's spine.

Chapter Thirty-Three

When Moore got back to the station, she found Burke in his office with Ann Quinlan. They both seemed to be very happy, laughing and joking together.

"Hi. What's the craic?"

"Hi, Fiona. Come on in. We're just celebrating. Ann has a full confession from both of those chancers downstairs. And better still, McNabb has gone off with his tail between his legs. Strike one for the Gardaí," Burke said.

"And don't forget Immigration, Inspector!"

"Of course not. Full marks. What about you Fiona? Anything new?"

"Na. I'll tell ya later. Well done, guys. Have they been charged with murder?"

"No, just people trafficking for now, but we've told the brief more charges are likely to follow. All done and dusted!"

"Great. Well, excuse me, I must get on."

Moore went and found Dónal Lawler and brought him fully up to speed on the interviews she had had with Emily McCranny and Darren Richardson.

"We need to bring Emily in again, and lean on her a bit. Richardson was lying through his teeth. He did it very well, but he was still lying."

"How do you know?"

"He's a real cool customer. Smooth as the proverbial, but I've dealt with enough of those types to know when they're peddling a story. I'm not saying they killed McCranny, but there's something not right," Moore said.

"Jesus, we better be careful, boss. You know what can go wrong if they think we are harassing bereaved relatives. Heffernan will jump all over it."

"Yes, but I'm pretty sure we're onto something here."

"If you say so, boss. When do you want to do it?"

"Let's leave it till the morning. I'm knackered anyway. Let's say we lift her at eight o'clock out in Foxrock."

"OK. Meet here at seven? Do you think she'll be home at eight?"

"Yep! When did you ever see a student up before eleven!"

Lawler laughed as Moore got her coat and left the station.

* * *

The following morning was dreary and wet. Moore had to set her windscreen wipers on double speed to clear the spray from the traffic in front of her. Overhead, heavy grey clouds ensured that the low winter sunrise stayed well away, making visibility difficult.

Moore rang the bell at McCranny's house and waited. There was no sound from within, so Moore rang again, as the drips from the awning in front of the door went down the back of her collar. After the third ring, the door was opened, and Janine appeared.

"Good morning, Janine. Sorry to call so early, but we need to speak to Emily," Moore said, looking around on the gravel to where a ten-year-old Fiat Punto was parked alongside her mother's Mercedes.

"There's no one up yet," Janine said defensively.

"Yes, I'm sorry it's so early, but we still need to see her. And could we step in out of the rain, do you think? I'm getting soaked here."

Janine stood back to allow the two detectives to enter the hallway. Moore wiped her feet thoroughly on the mat to emphasise the inclement weather outside.

"I suppose I better go and wake her then. But Mrs McCranny will be furious!" Janine said.

"That's you off her Christmas card list then," Dónal Lawler said to Moore when the girl had departed.

"When Emily comes down, let's not piss about. If she's not dressed, I'll go back up with her while she puts on her clothes. I don't want her phoning Darren Richardson. Then we'll take her back into Store Street. OK?" Moore said.

"Yeah, gotcha."

A few moments later, Emily McCranny came down the stairs in her dressing gown and slippers. Her hair was a mess, but even so, her natural good looks shone through.

"Good morning, Emily. This is Detective Garda Lawler. We need you to accompany us to Store Street Garda station. Could you get dressed, please," Moore said. "I'll come up with you while you get ready."

"What's this about? I thought I'd answered all your questions."

"Some new information has come to light. Now can we get on?" Moore said, moving towards the stairs.

The two women appeared a few minutes later. Emily had put on a pair of jeans and a loose-fitting top, and had dragged a brush through her hair, so she now looked even more radiant. As they moved towards the door, Emily said to Janine who was standing close by looking a bit confused, "Tell mum when she gets up where I've gone, won't you?"

"Yes. Of course."

There was virtually no conversation on the way back to the city. The traffic was dreadful, and it took them a full hour to complete the journey, much to the delight of Dónal Lawler who was seated in the back of the car beside Emily.

When they arrived, Emily was cautioned in the presence of the desk sergeant, who asked her to surrender her mobile phone. When the girl had been shown into an interview room, Moore asked Lawler to take the phone upstairs and download all the text and WhatsApp messages from it and print them out.

Moore went off to get a spot of breakfast while Lawler attended to the phone, and Emily settled in. She asked the desk sergeant to see if Emily wanted anything to eat or drink. Moore could get it from the Subway place around the corner.

Moore brought her breakfast roll and cardboard cup of coffee back to the open plan where Lawler was just finishing the printout from Emily McCranny's phone.

"Anything interesting?" Moore said.

"Most definitely. Have a look," he said, passing several A4 sheets with various speech bubbles imprinted on them across to her.

Moore studied the pages as she ate.

"Right. Do you want to sit in, Dónal?" Moore said.

"Shouldn't Inspector Burke be invited?"

"Na. He doesn't think she had anything to do with it. Let's surprise him!"

"Jesus, boss. You do like living dangerously, don't you?"

"Ah, it's just a bit of fun, Dónal. C'mon, let's do it!"

* * *

"Well, Emily, do you know why you are here?" Moore said, opening the interview.

"No, I don't. Why am I here?"

"We need to ask you some questions about the death of your father. Would you like to have a solicitor present?"

"Do I need one?"

"That's entirely up to you, Emily. But I can arrange a duty solicitor for you if you like," Moore said.

"No, it's OK. I'm fine. Thanks."

"OK. Now, these are the transcripts of messages exchanged between yourself and Darren Richardson on the night you entered your father's offices to use the office equipment."

Moore produced the A4 sheets that Lawler had printed off.

"In this message, you ask Darren if he had procured 'the stuff'. What stuff would that be, Emily?"

"Just stuff. Nothing special."

"I put it to you that the 'stuff' being referred to was in fact the arsenic that killed your father. Would that be right?"

Emily said nothing, but looked down at the top of the table and wrung her hands.

"And a few seconds later, you messaged Darren saying, 'bring it over. I'm here now. I'll let you in.' So, did Darren bring a quantity of arsenic to Mr McCranny's premises that night?"

Emily remained silent.

"You know, Emily, by not answering these questions, if this comes to court, a jury might interpret your silence as guilt. You really would be better to answer my questions."

The girl continued to remain quiet. Lawler tapped Moore's foot under the table, signalling that he wanted to have a go.

"Look, Emily," he said, leaning across the table and speaking softly, "we know that your father was killed by someone injecting his cigars with arsenic. And now we have these messages that could easily be interpreted as Darren Richardson having brought the poison to you whilst you were in your father's offices late at night. And you have easy access to needles and syringes from college. So, Emily, putting two and two together, you can see what we get."

Lawler sat back. A tense silence filled the room. Moore thought that the young detective might have disclosed too much information to their new principal suspect, but she was loath to speak first. In her experience, the next person to speak usually lost the argument.

"All right, all right! You've figured it all out. After I found him – my father – having sex with that thing in his office, I couldn't stand it. It disgusted me – my own father, my own flesh and blood – it was horrible. I couldn't get it out of my head. It just kept going round and round. I couldn't concentrate on my college work or anything. I talked to Darren about it, and we figured out what to do. Darren knew just what dose to administer, and where to get the stuff and everything."

Moore nodded to Lawler who took the hint and went off to bring Richardson in too.

"So, Emily, you are saying that Darren Richardson and yourself both plotted to kill your father, essentially because he was gay, and that you carried out that plan together, resulting in your father's death the same day that his car crashed, out on the road above Tallaght, is that right?"

"That's about it, Sergeant. What will happen to us?"

"That's not up to me to decide. You will be charged with conspiracy to murder on joint enterprise – that means both of you are equally to blame – and then a jury will decide your fate. But you should expect a custodial sentence, that's a certainty. Right, now we need to go out front while I formally charge you. We might be able to get you before a judge tomorrow, and I expect you will get bail till the trial."

"Does that mean I can go home?"

"Let's see."

Epilogue

Burke was unhappy when he learned that Moore and Lawler had wrapped up the murder of Gerald McCranny without him, but of course he couldn't show it. Instead, he congratulated them both through gritted teeth, and went upstairs to give Superintendent Heffernan the good news.

Heffernan was very pleased with the outcome, although he didn't really follow all the details of the matter completely, he was just glad to have the whole affair cleared up.

Taylor and Walsh were charged with a number of offences involving people trafficking, fraud and embezzlement, and were ultimately sentenced to five years, with the last year suspended. They would probably only serve twenty-four months. When they were released, they emigrated to France. Taylor got work easily enough doing drawings for house renovations and extensions all along the Loire Valley, and after a few years he re-qualified under the French code and set up an architectural practice.

On the basis of the excellent work done by Inspector Ann Quinlan, the evidence provided by Bilal Demir, and the information extracted from Taylor and Walsh, the French police were given several leads that enabled them to round up two gangs of traffickers and put a dent in the flow of illegal immigration from Turkey and other locations to the east.

Bilal Demir received the papers that would allow him to settle in Ireland. He also got leave to bring his wife across, and after a few months, he established his own maintenance business, providing plumbing and electrical services to householders. His work was good, and it wasn't long till he was constantly busy, earning good money.

Darren Richardson and McCranny's daughter, Emily, were tried for conspiracy to murder. Mitigation was provided by the defence counsel, who asserted that as they couldn't be certain that the dose they had administered in the cigars would definitely kill McCranny, the charge should be reduced. The two young students made a sorry sight in the dock at the trial, and quite quickly earned the sympathy of the jury as the details of McCranny's sexual exploits were outlined. The defence counsel also managed to introduce McCranny's use of what amounted to slave labour, so the victim's character was well blackened by the time the defence had made its case. When the jury retired to consider their verdict, almost fifty per cent of them were in favour of acquittal. But after several hours' deliberation, a majority verdict was reached, and Emily and Darren were found guilty of conspiracy to murder. They were sentenced to ten years each, with the last two years suspended.

Mrs McCranny was only moderately upset by the conviction of her daughter. She was a cold woman, with little emotional capacity. She put McCranny's companies up for sale, and by virtue of the valuable contracts the companies had, she achieved a handsome price. She is still living in the lap of luxury in Foxrock to this day.

Paddy Dunne was also convicted of murder. His defence argued that the balance of his mind was disturbed at the time of the crime. When the nature of his solitary and squalid lifestyle was explained, he too found sympathy in the twelve upright citizens who were to pass judgement on the man's crime. Before pronouncing sentence, the judge called for a psychiatric assessment to be carried out on Paddy, and eventually he was given five years in Dundrum – the institution for the criminally insane. He served his time, and when he was released, he returned to his old cottage which by this time had become totally uninhabitable. He spent a few months sleeping out in the various workmen's huts in the forest, but early in the following winter, which was severe, the cold took him and he passed away quietly in his sleep.

Character List

Detective Inspector Aidan Burke – a tough, and sometimes rough, detective from Dublin who is fond of a drink or two – or sometimes more.

Detective Sergeant Fiona Moore – Burke's assistant. She sometimes finds it hard to keep herself in check when Burke is in a grumpy mood.

Detective Garda Dónal Lawler – a keen young detective – the junior member of the team.

Superintendent Jerome Heffernan – a very wily Cork man with good international connections.

Inspector Ann Quinlan – a very competent member of the Immigration Department who is hoping for promotion.

Yves LeCroix – a senior French police officer who likes fine wine.

Melissa – a receptionist.

Sinéad Walsh – a very pretty, but devious young woman who is in a little over her head.

Freddy Taylor – a suave professional man. Architecture isn't his only qualification.

Bilal Demir – a Turkish immigrant whose family are still in Turkey.

Gerald McCranny – a wealthy business owner in the construction sector who enjoys a good Havana cigar.

Mrs McCranny – Gerald's wife.

Emily McCranny – the McCrannys' daughter, studying at Trinity College Dublin.

Janine – the McCranny's live-in au pair.

Darren Richardson – Emily McCranny's boyfriend.

Dr Malcolm O'Higgins – the state pathologist.

Dinny O'Leary – a woodsman who tends to the forestry plantation in the Dublin Mountains.

Paddy Dunne – Dinny O'Leary's side-kick.

Felix Lahart – a troubled young man, with issues about his sexuality.

Dr Terence Lahart – Felix's father.

If you enjoyed this book, please let others know by leaving a quick review on Amazon. Also, if you spot anything untoward in the paperback, get in touch. We strive for the best quality and appreciate reader feedback.

editor@thebookfolks.com

www.thebookfolks.com

ALSO IN THIS SERIES

Book I: A Deadly Dividend

A banker meets a lonely death. His girlfriend is targeted next. Who is on a killing spree and can DI Burke and DS Moore stop them?

OTHER BOOKS BY DAVID PEARSON

In the Galway Homicides series:

Murder on the Old Bog Road (Book 1)
Murder at the Old Cottage (Book 2)
Murder on the West Coast (Book 3)
Murder at the Pony Show (Book 4)
Murder on Pay Day (Book 5)
Murder in the Air (Book 6)
Murder at the Holiday Home (Book 7)
Murder on the Peninsula (Book 8)
Murder at the Races (Book 9)

Available in paperback and free with Kindle Unlimited

Printed in Great Britain
by Amazon

36053652R00123